FOREVER KIND OF COWBOY

Cowboy Dreamin' 5

I0519950

Sandy Sullivan

Erotic Romance

Secret Cravings Publishing
www.secretcravingspublishing.com

A Secret Cravings Publishing Book
Erotic Romance

Forever Kind of Cowboy
Copyright © 2014 Sandy Sullivan
Print ISBN: 978-1-63105-271-2

First E-book Publication: June 2014
First Print Publication: July 2014

Cover design by Dawné Dominique
Edited by Stephanie Balistreri
Proofread by Laurie White
All cover art and logo copyright © 2014 by Secret
Cravings Publishing

PUBLISHER
Secret Cravings Publishing
www.secretcravingspublishing.com

Dedication

This is for the fans of my cowboys.
I love you all!

For Angie Stanton-Johnson
Thank you for your feedback and friendship.
You're a doll!

FOREVER KIND OF COWBOY
Cowboy Dreamin' 5

Sandy Sullivan
Copyright © 2014

Chapter One

Callinda Marie Lewis glanced out the big bay doors of the gas station when Jeremiah Young pulled his truck up to the gas pump. Absent-mindedly, she swiped at the beads of sweat trickling down her neck heading for her shoulder blade and dropped her wrench from her wet palm in the process. The wrench hitting the cement under her feet made a loud clang. *Damn, it's hot today.* Or was it the man standing at the pump causing her to perspire?

As she picked up the tool, she noticed the jacked-up silver dually didn't fit Jeremiah's style from what she knew of the man. Ever since high school, he'd been the quiet Young brother, not too assuming and not one to draw attention, letting his brothers be the rowdy bunch. He crunched numbers on a daily basis. A whiz at math, he'd tutored her for a short time in algebra, but it hadn't lasted long enough for her. By then she'd been smitten.

Her heart thumped loudly in her chest as she tried to go back to work, denying the way she reacted to him. He always did this to her every time she saw him. From the moment he'd called her darlin' one day in high school, she couldn't think straight with him around. Her hands shook when she tried to ignore him standing at the pump in his Wranglers, cowboy hat, dusty boots, and button-down western shirt. "Why does he do this to me?"

"Callie?"

"Sorry, Dad. I'm just talking to myself."

Her father glanced out the bay doors and said, "Ah. I see." He set the carburetor down he'd been working on.

"It's nothin'."

"You've been tied up in knots about that boy for longer than I can remember." He patted her on the shoulder. "I understand, honey. I know what love feels like."

"It's not love, Dad. It's infatuation. That's all. He doesn't know I'm alive." Callie reached up to the bottom of the vehicle on the garage lift and pulled the plug to drain the oil from the engine, paying no mind to her dad moving to the other side of the car. She didn't want to see the look on his face. Ignoring the charismatic man outside was like forcing herself to stop breathing for minutes on end. It didn't happen without her feeling lightheaded.

"Why don't you go out there and see if he needs anything else besides gas?"

She wiped her hands on the rag she pulled from the back pocket of her coveralls. "I just might do that," she said, not taking her eyes off the well-built man standing near the pumps tapping his fingers on the bed of his truck.

Before she knew it, she stood next to him as he swung around, giving her a blinding smile. "Hey, darlin'."

Her toes curled in her steel-toed boots. "Hey, Jeremiah." She stuffed her hands in her pockets. "I thought I'd check to see if you needed anything else besides gas today? I could check your fluids, or somethin'."

"I think I'm good." Jeremiah reached up and wiped a smudge from her cheek. "You've been workin' hard today, huh?"

Her stomach knotted at the touch of his fingers on her face. God, she wished he'd touch her with passion, burying his hands in her long hair, pull it a little and crush his mouth to hers. "Uh, just changing old man Daniels' oil."

"Pretty girls shouldn't have grease smeared on their cheek." The pump made a clunking sound as it turned off. He turned to remove it from the gas tank on his truck and return it to the side of the pump.

"You sure I can't check your fluids for you?" *Wow, that sounded really desperate, you dummy.*

"Maybe next time. I have an appointment so I need to git, but I'll see you around."

"Sure. Thanks for coming in. We appreciate the business."

"Anytime, darlin'." He grasped the brim of his hat between his fingers, tipping it slightly as cowboys do. "I'll see you later." A soft whistling sound escaped his lips after he grinned and winked.

Several minutes later, he pulled out of the gas station, squealing his tires a little on the smooth pavement.

Her heart rate slowed as he went down the road then pulled into the diner his aunt owned. When he jumped out of his truck again, she couldn't help but sigh the second he swept Lydia Wiley up in his arms in a twirling hug. After her feet hit the ground, he brushed his lips against the girl's, earning himself an unseen frown from Callie. She didn't realize he was seeing Lydia, but then again, when wasn't he seeing someone?

Callie turned her back on the scene to walk into the garage. She'd seen enough to know she'd never have a chance with Jeremiah Young in this lifetime. Her type didn't get the gorgeous hunk of a man. That only happened in fairy tales and her life wasn't a fairy tale by any means.

Losing her mom at a young age didn't help. Her dad did the best he could. But being the only child raised by a man had her dressing and acting like a boy while enjoying things like dirt bikes, working on cars, and doing general tomboy stuff. She tied her hair back in a low ponytail just to keep it off her face. Dresses didn't do anything for her. Although once in a while, she broke down and wore something feminine to feel like a woman.

She wished she knew more about how things were supposed to work between two people when she'd given her virginity to David Burger in high school. The experience sucked. Never mind it had happened in the bed of his truck with very little foreplay involved. Somehow she knew things would be different with a man she cared about or one who knew how to handle a woman.

A sigh escaped her in a rush. She just knew someday things would be different. They had to be. She didn't want to spend the rest of her life alone.

* * * *

Jeremiah Young stared out the window of the diner as Lydia prattled on about something or another. Why did woman talk nonstop sometimes? Was it just to hear themselves yap about one thing only to change subjects and go on about something totally different?

"Are you even listening to me, Jeremiah?"

"Yeah," he answered automatically while his gaze fixed on the garage across the street. Callie Lewis moved through the double bay doors in her overalls and boots. Nothing specific to indicate she was a woman in any sense of the word except when she took her hair down and shook it out before putting it back up in the ever-present low ponytail. He'd known her since high school when he'd tutored her in algebra. They'd been in the same classes most of their lives including phys ed. He'd noticed her right away although she wasn't the type he normally took a second glance at. She didn't have huge tits nor was she particularly thin. Curvy would be the word he used for her. Nice curves, but she hid them under long T-shirts, baggy jeans and work boots most of the time. Once in a great while, he would see her in woman's clothes, something pretty like when she went to church on Sundays. The garage was closed those days while she spent the day with her dad. They would go out for Sunday supper at his aunt's diner. He always seemed to be driving by when they went in, not that he'd been looking or anything.

His cell phone beeped indicating an incoming message. He smiled as he checked his phone. As the financial planner of his parents' ranch, he had to keep his pulse on the bank accounts, investments, and inner workings of the ranch at all times. One of the stocks he'd invested heavily in with his own money had doubled today on the market. Good. He would make a tidy profit if it kept increasing before he sold it off.

Investments had been one of his past times since he could remember. He'd started running numbers in his own stocks from the time he'd turned eighteen, then he was careful with the family fortune when he chose to broaden the horizons on their behalf. His parents' trust in his ability to keep them afloat came with a heavy load. If he lost it all, they would be out on a limb, but he'd been lucky. So far, everything he'd put their money into had done well on the market. His own little nest egg seemed to be growing quite well. At this rate, he'd be able to retire soon.

Not that he didn't love his family or the ranch he'd grown up on, but he wanted to be financially stable enough to do his own thing rather than riding rough stock for the rest of his life.

Lydia jabbered on about something to do with her dress, or shoes, so he focused his gaze back out the window.

The town of Bandera, Texas wasn't much to look at, but it was home. His family moved there before he was born. They proceeded to run a cattle ranch as each of his eight brothers came into the world. His parents never had the daughter his mother craved. She made do with the ever-growing number of daughters-in-law and grandchildren as each of his brothers found their life mate. He wasn't sure what the hoopla was all about. One girl for the rest of his life? He wasn't into that quite yet. He had too much living to do. He wanted to see the world a little at a time. Go to Paris, live on the east coast somewhere, see Los Angeles, Seattle, San Francisco, Florida, and maybe even New York. He thought it would be totally cool to see the New York Stock Exchange one day since he dabbled so much in stocks now. Plus, someday he wanted a fancy sports car to zip around in. A Ferrari, or maybe a Lamborghini. What the hell he would do with it in Bandera, Texas he wasn't sure, but having one might be fun. To have so much money he'd never have to work again seemed to always be at the forefront of his mind.

"And this thong was so cute, Jeremiah. You would have loved it on me." Lydia's voice dropped to a whisper. "Or off."

"I'm sure."

She continued to talk as she stirred her Coke with the straw. Her voice faded out when he saw Callie walk across the main road of town headed for the diner. *Must be lunchtime.*

The bell over the door dinged when Callie walked in. Jeremiah kept her in view the whole time as she approached the counter to place her order. Her voice soothed the grating of Lydia's on his nerves. The sing-song lilt sounded so good to his ears.

"Jeremiah?"

"Sorry. What did you say?"

"I knew you weren't listening. What did I say last then?"

"Something about a thong."

"I said that ten minutes ago." Lydia glanced over her shoulder, catching the direction of his gaze. "Really?"

"What?"

"You're looking at Callinda Lewis?" She snorted—actually snorted.

He thought it was funnier than hell. Laughter burst from his lips, earning him a frown from Lydia.

Callie turned toward him for a moment, stuffing her hands in her pockets as she hunched her shoulders.

"She's really not your type, you know. She doesn't even own a dress from what I hear, and makeup? Forget it."

"She doesn't need it."

"Yes, she does. A woman doesn't go out of the house without makeup. It's just not womanly. The mere thought is as hideous as those clothes are." She leaned back in her chair, sipping on her drink a minute before she continued. "She works in her father's garage, for God's sake. A woman doesn't work on cars, dress in overalls, drink beer or cuss like a sailor."

"What about her bugs you, Lydia?" He rapped his knuckles on the table. "That men actually look at her while you're in the room?"

"Look at her? Really, Jeremiah. She's nothing to look at."

"I think she is. She's got something you don't have."

"What's that?"

"A personality beyond everything revolving around her. She doesn't care if she's all decked out in a pretty dress. She cares about the people around her. She's not all about herself, like you are."

Lydia jumped to her feet. "Then go out with her!"

Jeremiah smiled. "I'm glad you give your permission although it's not needed, but thank you anyway. I'll do that." He got to his feet and walked toward Callie as she stood there openmouthed. "I could kiss you right now." Her blue eyes were wide as her mouth hung open like she was ready to catch flies with it, so he put a finger under her chin to push it closed. "Easy, darlin'. I won't. Not yet at least."

"Wha…what?"

"I think you'd be a bit shocked if I did, so how about this? Will you go out to dinner and a movie with me on Friday?" he asked, smirking a little as he glanced back at Lydia.

Lydia jammed her hands on her hips as she glared. "You're a bastard, Jeremiah. No wonder no woman will have you for long," she yelled before she stormed out of the diner.

Jeremiah turned his attention back to Callie. "So what do you say?"

"To?"

"Going out with me on Friday?"

"You weren't serious, were you?"

"Of course, I am. So what do you say?"

"Uh, okay."

"I'll pick you up at your dad's house at six?"

"Sounds fine to me."

"Great." He tipped his hat and said, "I'd invite you to have lunch with me, but I need to get on back to the ranch. I'll see you Friday." He slipped his aunt a ten dollar bill for the hassle before he stepped out into the sunshine of the day, whistling softly as he headed for his truck.

The drive back to the home place went by rather quickly as he let his thoughts wander to Callie. He'd wanted to ask her out for some time, but for some reason he'd never found the opportunity. Well, that wasn't really true. He stopped into the gas station at least once a week whether he needed gas or not, just to see her.

She was a total enigma to him. Real, not made up to be something she wasn't. Liked the same things he liked, fishing, hunting, cars, four-wheeling, and beer, which made her even more fascinating.

Every Friday night, she met with a few of her friends at The Dusty Boot, got a little drunk and then went home. She didn't go home with anyone from what he'd seen of her escapades. Maybe she went to San Antonio for her fun. *Hell, maybe she's a virgin.* The thought brought a frown to his lips. He didn't do virgins. Things got messy with a woman who didn't like sex the way he did. Not that he was weird about sex. Well, maybe a little. He did like variety.

The ranch came into view a few minutes later as he pulled up the gravel drive to the gate. Once he punched in the numbers, the wrought iron gate slowly opened, allowing him entrance onto the property.

Longhorn cattle grazed in the distance to his left when he drove up the long, winding drive to approach the main lodge. The multi-story building was half stone, half wood with three big dormer windows in the front looking out over the yard. A huge porch graced the area with several rockers and benches for guests to sit and enjoy the sunset if they wish.

Jeremiah did a double-take as he noticed the old cowboy sitting in one of the rockers for a second before he disappeared into thin air. The ghosts around the property gave him the shivers sometimes when they made noise or appeared out of nowhere, but most of the time he tried to ignore them.

As he approached the front of the lodge and pushed open the door, he was met by one of the kitchen workers coming out to ring the lunch bell. The guests on the ranch were summoned to meals by the ringing of the steel bell hanging on the hook outside the door.

"Oh hey, Jeremiah," Mandy said as she reached up to grab the rope hanging from the end of the bell.

"Hi, Mandy."

Mandy had been a friend of Paige and Peyton's who now worked on the ranch serving the meals three times a day. She also helped Paige with the twins who were born almost a year ago. Wow, time sure did fly these days. Getting old sucked.

"I thought you were in town?" She clanged the bell three times.

Several people came out of their little cabins and headed toward them. Meals were a very social event at the ranch, one he enjoyed a lot. The different people who came to stay there always made for interesting conversations. Many times, he would sit at a table with some of tourists so he could talk with them. He liked learning about different places. It gave him a mental list of the sights he'd like to see someday. "I was, but I'm home now."

"Are you going to be working this afternoon?"

"Yeah. I guess. I hadn't planned on it, but since my day is messed up, I might as well. Why?"

"Do you think you could help me? I've got some college algebra to do and I just don't get it."

"Sure. Come by my office between the meals when you have some time and I'll help you."

"Thanks. You're a doll."

He leaned in to hug her quickly before the crowd made it to the steps. "Don't tell the ladies. I won't be able to beat them off with a stick I keep behind the door."

"You are too much."

He grinned as he stepped back to allow the guests to enter the lodge for the noon meal. "When are you going to wrangle one of my brothers into marryin' you?"

She laughed as she punched him in the arm. "I'm workin' on it."

He liked Mandy, not the way one would like a girl they were interested in, but like a sister. She'd been an instrumental part of Peyton getting away from her crazy ex and finding her way to being in love with his brother, Jason. He liked that his brothers were pairing up with some really great gals. Maybe it was time for him to settle down too after all.

"I need to get back to work before your mom fires my ass."

Jeremiah chuckled. "Like that's going to happen. You're good for this place."

"Well thank you, kind sir. I love my job and hanging out with you all. It's like a home away from home." She walked with him toward the serving tables. "I'll talk to you after the meal is served and we get the dishes done."

"Okay. Find me in my office." The family table had to be divided into two tables with the addition of all the women in the house.

He noticed an empty spot on the end where Joshua normally sat. He glanced around to find his brother sitting with a pretty, blonde woman at one of the other tables. Maybe the lone, unattached triplet was finding one of his own? He hoped so.

Jeremiah took the empty chair, turning it backward and straddling it with his thighs much to the chagrin of his mother, who frowned from across the table.

"We sit like adults at this table, Jeremiah."

He stood up to turn the chair the right way before he eased his large frame into the seat. Leave it his mother to make him feel like an eight-year-old again. He loved her to pieces, but sometimes she drove him nuts. "Sorry, Mom." His cell phone beeped again. After he removed it from the holster at his hip, he checked the message to see the final stock report for the day. He smiled. Things were looking up.

"No phone at the table, Jeremiah."

"Yes, Mom. Sorry. I had to check on my stock report."

"You know the rules."

"I'll go put it in my office. Be right back." *Damn.* Chastised by his mother at the table, but Nina Young ruled the house with an iron fist and her sons knew it. He should have ignored the urge to immediately answer the beep. Most of the time he could get away with leaving his phone in the holster, but checking it at the table was a no-no.

He opened his office door and flipped on the computer screen for a second as he laid his phone on the desk. The stock report came up immediately when the monitor turned on. A grin spread across his face as his portfolio just took a huge jump with the purchase of the climbing stocks. If he sold in the next couple of days, he would be able to retire on his gains. He pumped his fist into the air a couple of times.

"You coming back to the table?" Jeff asked as he walked by the door.

"Yeah. Be right there."

"You're in a good mood."

"Yep. Financial stability will do that for you."

"That's awesome, Jeremiah. Now if you'd find a good woman to settle down with, you'd be all set."

"Don't put the cart before the horse there, brother." He slapped Jeff on the back as they walked back out toward the dining room together. "We all can't be as happy as you are. How's Terri feeling?"

"A lot better with this pregnancy than the last, although I wish we hadn't added to the family so soon."

"It'll be okay. James is two."

"I know. I just hope it's a girl this time."

"Having boy problems?"

"Ben is getting very mouthy lately. He starts school this fall and I'm afraid the teachers are going to have lots of problems with his back talking."

"He'll be fine. He's his daddy's son."

"That's what I'm afraid of.

Chapter Two

Friday evening rolled around, bringing with it tension and apprehension for Callie. Her shoulders bunched with anxiety, her hands were sweating, her heart raced around her chest like a horse running the Kentucky Derby, and her whole body shuddered with nerves. What the hell was she thinking agreeing to a date with Jeremiah?

"Easy, girl." Her stomach flipped. Yeah, she'd been on dates before, but not with the man she'd lusted after for several years. *Lusted after. That was one way to put it.* She wouldn't agree with her heart when the stubborn organ whispered she was in love with him. She couldn't be. He hardly knew she existed. Besides, she definitely wasn't his type. He went out with skinny, model-thin women, not the rather rounded, plump-figured girls like her. Her boobs were too small, her waist too thick, her legs too rounded and her butt? Wow, don't get her started on her butt. So why did he ask her out? "Just to piss off Lydia, I'm sure."

Like Lydia would care.

Callie glanced at the clock before looking down at the slinky red number she wore. It hugged her curves to perfection, showing off her hourglass figure. This would show off everything she owned. She didn't even know where they were going or what they were going to do, but she felt the need to knock his socks off with her dress. If tart was what he wanted, tart would be what he got. She smoothed her hands over the skirt, looking down at the red high heels on her feet. Her toes looked hideous peeking out of the ends of the shoes, but at least she'd done the girlie thing painting them a bright red to go with her dress. Maybe she should have had a pedicure done. She snorted as she covered her mouth with her hand. Yeah, right. She *had* put on a little makeup and curled her hair. The main attraction was the dress though. She planned to knock him dead with this outfit.

The doorbell rang precisely on time for Jeremiah's arrival.

"I'll get it," her father called from the living room. "Hi, Jeremiah. How are you tonight?"

Voices carried through her partially closed bedroom door. She was ready, but she felt the need to gather her courage a bit before she went into the front room. Not having a mother past her third birthday didn't bode well for being all that feminine, but her aunt had tried raising her up right with all the girly things. Callie didn't care much for it growing up though. She liked working with her dad, going fishing, going hunting, riding dirt bikes, and four-wheelers. All the things girls weren't supposed to enjoy. Tonight she would be the woman Jeremiah went tongue-tied over.

"She'll be out in a minute, son. Have a seat. Can I get you something to drink?"

The rumble of Jeremiah's voice sent shivers racing across her arms. "No, sir. I'm fine. Thank you."

"How are things at your parent's place?"

"Keeping us hopping, although the season is coming to an end."

"True, true. How is the cattle business treating you all?"

"We manage to stay afloat. The guest ranch keeps things moving. We are booked solid through most of the winter even though the weather doesn't give them much to do on a ranch. They still come for the good old-fashioned hospitality, home-cooking, and southern charm."

"I hear you are making yourself a name on the stock market with your trading."

"That right?"

"Yep."

"Do you trade?"

"I dabble. Nothing like you, I'm afraid."

"It's all in the numbers."

"I'm sure. You'll have to let me in on a few you've got going. I'd love to be able to make sure Callie doesn't have to work at the station for the rest of her life to have a home."

"Sure, Mr. Lewis. We can talk more about it tomorrow if you'd like to meet me for lunch?"

"Certainly, Jeremiah. Thanks."

Callie took it as her cue to come out of her room even though she really didn't want to. She was afraid to meet Jeremiah's gaze as she rounded the end of the couch and came into his view, but she shouldn't have been. The appreciation shining in his gaze, as he got to his feet, warmed her soul.

His jaw dropped as she wobbled slightly on the four-inch heels. "Well?"

"Wow. You look fabulous."

"Thanks." She smoothed the tight skirt a little around her thighs. "It's nothing special, but I wasn't sure where we were going, so I didn't know how to dress."

"It's perfect." He took her hand and brought it to his mouth to kiss the back of her fingers.

Holy hell, I'm in trouble.

"You two kids have fun. Be home before midnight."

"Dad!"

Her father laughed as her face flushed red.

"I'm kidding."

"Let me grab my bag. Oh, and my phone."

"Sure."

She rushed back into her bedroom to grab a few things. In a hurried thought, she grabbed two condoms from her nightstand drawer, shoving them into the zippered pocket of her purse before she headed back out to meet Jeremiah in the living room. *I can hope, can't I?*

Jeremiah slid her hand into his as they walked toward the door of her dad's house and then out to his truck. Again, she was struck by how the vehicle didn't suit him although he was a cowboy to the bone with his Wranglers, western shirt, boots, and cowboy hat, she thought there had to be more to him than met the eye.

"What?" he asked as he opened the door for her.

"I always thought you would be more comfortable in a sports car than a truck like your brothers."

He shut the door on her side before walking around the front to get into the driver's side. "You know, one of my dreams is to own a foreign sports car."

She laughed as she turned in the seat to face him. "Why am I not surprised at all. Let me guess. Ferrari."

"That's one of them, yep."

"I can just see you zipping around the back roads of Bandera in your car."

He cranked the engine of his truck over with a twist of the key. The diesel rumbled to life, sending a little thrill through her body. She had a thing for engines in general, but a diesel always ramped her up. Over the years, her dad had taught her to work on all kinds of cars at the garage. There wasn't an engine he couldn't fix, although with the newer cars, it had become more and more difficult for him to make any money at the garage. She hoped things got better soon. Otherwise, they might lose the station.

"Where are we going?"

"I thought we'd get some Tex-Mex at the River Walk in San Antonio and then hit a nice little club I know."

"Okay."

"You do like Mexican food, right?"

"Love it. One of my favorites."

"Good." He glanced across the cab of the truck as they pulled onto the highway headed for the city. "Did I tell you how gorgeous you look tonight?"

"Sort of, but thank you."

"I've never seen you in a dress like that, I think. You usually are more conservative like what you were wearing last Sunday."

"Last Sunday?"

"Yeah, I usually see you with your dad going to Sunday brunch at the diner after church."

"You do?"

"Yes. You look real nice."

She bit the inside of her cheek so she wouldn't ask why he noticed her on Sundays going into the diner. Surely he wasn't that interested in her, right?

"You smell right nice too."

Boy, is he doling out the compliments tonight. What gives? "It's okay, Jeremiah. I know you only asked me out to piss off Lydia, so you might as well take me back home right now rather than go through with this date thing. I'm not the kind of woman you normally go out with and I'm sure taking me in San Antonio is just so you don't have to show up with me at the diner of somewhere else where we might be seen. This is ridic—"

Jeremiah slammed on the breaks, pulling the truck over to the side of the road. When he jammed the gearshift on the truck into park, she pushed her back against the door, a little afraid of what he might do. Fury and frustration made his face look like granite. His eyebrows drew down, making them look slashed above angry grey eyes. She'd never seen Jeremiah Young pissed off before. She wasn't sure she wanted to again.

"Enough. I did not ask you out because I wanted to piss Lydia off. I don't care what she thinks. All I care about is what you think. Whether you believe me or not, I wanted to take you out. I have for a long time. I just didn't have the guts to ask. You're a very beautiful woman and I like you the way you are."

"You wanted to ask me out?"

"Yes. We've known each other a long time, Callie. You aren't the type of woman I usually go out with. You're more of a permanent relationship type girl. I'm not sure I'm ready for that kind of thing. You aren't the type to fuck and walk away from. That scares the hell out of me, which is why I never asked you out before."

"I'm not?" She shook her head. "I mean, no I'm not, but I could be if that's what you wanted." Desperation riddled her subconscious. She wanted him on any terms she could get him even if it was only for one night.

"You would become something you aren't for me?"

"Yes." She blew out a long breath. "I've wanted you for a long time, Jeremiah. I can be whatever you want me to be for however long you want me. No hearts or feelings will get into the mix. I promise."

He swallowed rather hard, his Adam's apple bobbing a couple of times before he spoke again. "Are you propositioning me for a one-nighter?"

"Yes."

"And the rules of this fling?"

"We have one great night, no feelings get involved. We part as friends."

He tapped his fingers on the steering wheel for a minute before he pushed his hat back on his head and turned to look at her. "One night?"

The grey of his eyes turned stormy in the fading light of the evening. Labor Day would be on them soon. The summer would be coming to a close. Winter in Bandera always seemed long and lonely to her. She wished for more than one night, but if that's all there was, then so be it. "Yes. I'm game for one night of hot sex with you."

"You really want to do this?"

"Yep. What do you say?"

A rough exhale pierced the silence of the cab. "Let's have dinner. We can decide for sure at the end of the evening. Who knows, maybe we aren't even compatible."

Like hell. Judging from how I react to your touch, if we aren't compatible, I'll eat my shoe. "Sounds good to me."

He nodded once, put the truck into gear and pulled out into traffic as Callie contemplated what she'd just done. A deal with the devil, no doubt, and she was sure she'd get burned in the process. One night of mind-blowing sex with Jeremiah Young. What could go wrong?

* * * *

Jeremiah parked the truck along the narrow road near the San Antonio River Walk so they could take a stroll down the sidewalk to the restaurant he wanted to take Callie to. He wasn't sure if she'd ever been to this particular restaurant, but it was one of his favorites and they even had a mariachi band that played while the diners ate.

The evening breeze blew softly through the area, cooling things down from the heat of the afternoon sun. Lights bathed each restaurant in a soft glow as they approached the one he'd made reservations for.

"Young, party of two."

"Ah, yes sir. One moment please and I'll have your table ready."

"Thank you."

They stood side by side, not touching, but shifting from foot to foot as they waited for the hostess to seat them. He hadn't said anything more about her crazy scheme on the ride into the city as he continued to roll it over in his mind. It was the perfect scenario, but somehow he just knew things would go wrong in the end. However, he'd never had trouble walking away from a woman before, so he shouldn't with Callie, right? Of course not. His heart and his head hadn't interfered in the past. They would have some great sex and get the urge out of their systems, he hoped. Still being able to see other people when things were said and done seemed like a great idea to him.

"Right this way, please."

He laid the palm of his hand at the small of her back as they followed the hostess through the tables toward the patio area up on the second floor.

"Will this be all right, sir?"

"Perfect. Thank you." Callie rubbed her arms as if chilled, so he took off the suit jacket he wore to drape it over her shoulders. "Can't have you getting chilled with your shoulders bare."

"Thank you."

"You're welcome." He held out her chair while he waited for her to sit before taking his own across from her. He wanted to be able to look into her gorgeous blue eyes while they sipped margaritas and ate chips.

"You're such a gentleman."

"My mother would be proud to hear you say so. She raised us boys right, I guess."

"I would say so." Callie laid the napkin on her lap before she picked up the menu. "Hmm. What sounds good besides having you for supper?"

He wasn't sure he heard her right. "Would you like a margarita?"

"I suppose, although something a bit stronger would certainly loosen things up in the nether regions."

Jeremiah ordered her one and a Jack and Coke for himself when the waitress stopped at their table.

"I'll have one of what he's having instead of the margarita."

"Of course. I'll be right back with your drinks," the waitress said, sliding the tortilla chips and salsa onto the table between them.

He must have had a startled look on his face because she said, "What?"

"I figured you for one of those fruity drink kind of gals."

"I'm feeling right adventurous tonight."

"Apparently." As he perused the menu, he kept glancing over the top to look at the woman across the table from him. He couldn't believe this was the same sweet girl he'd tutored in math in high school. Sure, he'd talked to her, saw her, and watched her off and on since they graduated several years ago, but he hadn't seen her like this.

"Is there something on my nose?" she asked, setting her menu down on the table to her left before she grabbed a chip, dipped it into the salsa and then popped it between those tempting as hell lips.

"No. Why?"

"You're staring."

"Sorry. I'm trying to figure out what happened to the Callinda Lewis I know, because I think you left her back at your house. I don't know this girl at all."

"What's wrong with me being different than the girl you grew up with?"

"Nothing, but I like Callie too. Is this Callie or Callinda?"

"It's me, Jeremiah. I'm not any different than the girl you've known your whole life, but you haven't been out with me on a date. This is how I am."

"Somehow I don't think so. Don't put on a different persona for me. I liked you the way you were."

"You don't like this me?"

"It's not that. I think this you is hotter than holding a firecracker, but the sweet Callie is nice too."

The waitress brought their drinks and then took their order for food. The evening darkness had started to surround them as the sun went down. Candles were lit on the tabletops covered with brightly colored tablecloths. The light flickering from the small candle made her eyes sparkle like sapphires. He hadn't noticed their deep blue color before or how kissable her lips were.

"I'm not a virgin, you know. I've been around a bit. Dabbled in some bondage. Nipple clamps, rope work, dildos…that kind of thing."

He choked on the sip of his drink he'd just swallowed. "Oh?"

Her lips bowed into a teasing little smile. "No. I lost it in high school so you don't have to worry about my inexperience."

After a couple of coughs, he said in a gravelly voice laced with the whiskey he'd practically choked on, "I really hadn't thought about it."

"Well I have. I wish it had been you."

"Callie—"

"Am I making you uncomfortable?"

"A little. I'm not used to you being this bold."

"You don't like bold women?" she asked, sipping her own drink with a wide-eyed expression that made her look all the more innocent except the dark eyeliner she rimmed her eyes with.

This Callie had him stumped. He wasn't sure what to make of the changes in her and he wasn't sure he liked it at all. Of course, he liked bold women to an extent, but this didn't fit the Callie he knew. "I do."

"So what's the problem?"

Their food arrived, saving him from trying to explain his thoughts to her. Was she trying to impress him? Make him want her over Lydia? Didn't she realize he'd much rather go out with her than Lydia?

They ate for several minutes in silence as he tried to think of how to approach this. He didn't want to put Callie off, but he wanted the old Callie, not this new throw herself in your face girl sitting across the table from him.

"You aren't eating. Aren't you hungry?"

He looked down at this plate and true, he'd been shoving his food around with his fork more than he'd been eating his enchilada. Placing the fork to the side, he tented his fingers so he could watch her. "I guess not so much."

A blush spread across her cheeks as she glanced down at her own plate. "The food is wonderful. I'm glad you brought me here. I haven't been to this one before, although I've been down on the River Walk thousands of times."

"This one is my favorite restaurant. I come here as much as I can when I'm in town."

The mariachi band strolled by their table to ask if they wanted them to play a song. After Jeremiah gave them a tip, they played a soft Mexican ballad meant for lovers. A moment later, he felt her foot slide along his inner thigh, heading for his crotch. *Holy hell!* "Listen, Callie." He shoved her foot down. "This is moving a bit fast for me."

"What's wrong?" She swallowed hard, looking like she was about to cry. "I'm coming on too strong, aren't I? I'm sorry. I'm totally embarrassed now."

"It's okay. This just isn't the girl I know. I'm sorry, but I'm not sure I like her very much."

"Wow."

"I'm finished if you want me to take you home." He signaled the waitress for the check as he pulled his wallet out of his pants pocket.

"I guess so."

The moment he paid for their tab, he stood to escort her back to his truck. This whole date had turned into a disaster and he wasn't sure what to think about it. Obviously, he didn't know her as well as he thought he did because man, this Callie wasn't for him. She made Lydia look like a saint. That was hard to do since Lydia was a bitch.

Silence stretched between them on the ride home. They didn't talk at all and he thought he heard her sniffle several times like she might be crying, but he didn't know what to do. If he played it like it was okay, he'd feel like a heel because he'd led her on. He didn't want the girl she'd been at dinner. He wanted the sweet Callie he'd known all his life. He wasn't sure how to find the real girl.

Chapter Three

I'm such an idiot! Callie felt like shit. She'd totally screwed up this date with Jeremiah. She probably wouldn't get a chance with him again and didn't know how to fix this. Trying to be the woman she thought he liked turned out to be the last thing he wanted. What to do? "Jeremiah, I'm sorry."

"For what?"

"Acting like a prima donna or whatever you want to call it. I thought you like those kind of women."

"No. Yes." He raked his fingers through his hair as they pulled up to the curb in front of her house. "I'm not sure what I like at this point, Callie, but I know the woman you were at dinner tonight wasn't what I wanted. I liked you the way you were. Sweet, innocent, tomboyish. It's nice to be with a woman who isn't all about the hair and makeup. You work on cars. You like to go fishing and four-wheelin'. Those are the things I like about you." He shut the truck off before he turned to face her. "I don't need to jump into bed with you on the first date either. Not that I wouldn't mind, but it's not what this is about. I want to get to know you as the girl I went to high school with who has turned into this hottie."

"Hottie?" she asked, blushing to the roots of her hair. He thought she was hot? *Wow*.

"Yeah." He took her hand and threaded his fingers through hers. "I like you the way you are. Don't change."

"Okay." She loved the feeling of her hand in his. Warmth spread up her arm, making her heart flutter in her chest. She had it bad for this man, always had. "Can we start over?"

"Sure."

She captured her bottom lip between her teeth as she tried to think of how to start this whole night again without the act. Once she unbuckled her seatbelt, she turned to face him. "How was your day today?"

His lips lifted in a half grin as he began telling her all about what he did at the ranch, how his stocks were doing, and everything about his life as the Young brother in charge of the finances. Her heart warmed as she relayed everything about her day. They almost sounded like an old married couple as they talked. She told him about working on the transmission she'd been having trouble with at the garage, how the same customers came in every week for gas, including him, and how she enjoyed spending Sundays with her dad going to church before they went out for Sunday dinner at his aunt's diner.

"She enjoys having you for supper, I'm sure."

"It's just me and Dad time, so it's fun. We talk about all kinds of things." She scooted closer. "Tell me what it was like growing up with such a huge family."

"I forgot you were an only child."

"Yeah. When Mom left us, Dad had to do what he could. He didn't know how to raise a girl."

"He did a damn good job. I don't know many women out there who can do what you do. It's a great trait to have." He brought her hand to his lips, brushing the back lightly. "You are an amazing woman, Callie."

She smiled at the compliment, absorbing everything about being with Jeremiah she could. Talking to him about little things made this the best date ever. "Would you like to come in?" She glanced at the front of the house, watching as her dad's light in his bedroom went out. "Dad went to bed so we can sit and watch a movie here since we didn't hit the theater."

"Okay. Do you have some popcorn?"

She gave him her best *are you crazy* look and said, "What is a movie without popcorn?"

With a tip of his head, he pushed open the driver's side door before slamming it shut. She waited for him to come around to open her door and help her out of the truck, knowing it was what men like Jeremiah did.

When they stopped at the door of the house for her to open it, he rested his hand at the small of her back. The warmth emanating from his skin sent goose bumps down her legs. She knew he probably only did it because he was raised to be a gentleman, but she loved having him touch her. "Let me check in with Dad for a minute. There are movies on television or you can pick one of the discs we have in the entertainment center."

"Okay."

She headed down the hall to tap on her father's door. Since he'd seen the light go off only a few minutes before, she figured she should at least let him know she was home. "Dad?"

"Come in."

"We're back."

He glanced at the clock on the bedside table. "It's early."

"I know. We decided to watch a movie here instead of going out."

"All right. You two kids have fun."

"We will. I love you, Daddy."

"I love you too, doll baby. Be good."

She laughed. "I'll try." After she closed the door behind her, she walked down the long hall toward the kitchen to make the popcorn and get them something to drink.

Jeremiah was still looking through the discs when she glanced across the island. "What would you like to drink?"

"Anything cold is fine."

"I have Coke?"

He looked back at her with a grin on his perfect lips. "Perfect!"

She poured him a glass with some ice in it as she kicked off the heels on her feet. With a heavy sigh, she leaned on the bar with her elbow.

"You okay?"

"Yeah, but those heels were killing me."

He set the discs he was looking at down and walked around the island. "You didn't have to do all of this for me."

"I thought you liked those kinds of women."

"Sometimes, but like I said, I like the Callie I already knew. I just want to get to know her better." His gaze raked down her body, causing her nipples to pull into tight little nubs under her dress. "Although you look killer in that dress."

Her cheeks heated with a blush as she set the can down on the counter. "Thanks."

He leaned in to kiss her on the forehead. "Why don't you change into something more comfortable like sweats and a T-shirt?"

Her whole body shivered from the touch of his lips. She really wanted them on hers. Once would be enough, right? Yeah, probably not, but she could live for the moment. "Really?"

"Yes. I like seeing your curves in that clingy little number, but I know it can't be very comfortable."

He'd noticed her curves, wow. "It's not."

He swatted her on the butt as she started to walk toward her room. "Then go change, woman, and I'll get the popcorn in the microwave."

The moment she had a second for herself, she leaned against the closed door and sighed. He'd kissed her even if it was just on the forehead—she'd had Jeremiah's lips on her skin. Why did he have to be the one to turn her upside down like this? Why did it have to be one of the Young brothers? Why not someone easy to love? Not them. They all were bachelors to the core. Well, until they met the right woman. A few of the boys had settled down recently, but all of them were women from somewhere besides here. Bandera, Texas residents weren't what the boys looked for when they contemplated a mate, or at least it appeared so. "They're attracted to a different woman, not some down-home country girl like me." Oh well. She'd take what she could get. For tonight, Jeremiah Young was all hers.

After she quickly changed into a pair of shorts and a T-shirt, she did a quick swipe of a makeup cloth to get the majority of the goop off her face. She'd done herself up with dark eyeliner, lipstick and all, thinking he liked women all dolled up. It turns out he didn't want it at all. Who knew? If she compared herself to Lydia, she came up lacking. She didn't do her hair on a regular basis, she didn't wear makeup all that much, and she didn't dress fancy. With a glance in the mirror behind her door, she screwed up her mouth in a twist of a sarcastic smile before she opened the door so she could head back into the living room.

"Now there's the girl I know and love."

Love?

Jeremiah patted the couch next to him as he settled the full bowl of popcorn on his thigh. "You look like what I picture you always wearing. I bet you're more comfortable too."

"Yeah, I am. This is what I wear most of the time during the summer."

He looked at her legs with a crooked grin as he tossed a couple of kernels of popcorn into his mouth. "Nice legs."

"What? These old things?" She plopped down on the couch beside him, almost spilling the popcorn.

"Easy, woman! The popcorn!"

The peal of his laughter made her smile. She loved his laugh. Hell, she loved everything about him.

"Sorry." She grabbed a few pieces for herself as she asked, "What did you pick out?"

"*Die Hard.*"

"Of course."

"Hey, it's an action flick, but it has the mushy stuff too. I mean, you know how he hollers his wife's name and everything."

She rolled her eyes. "It's so not a woman's kind of movie. *Love Actually, You've Got Mail,* those kinds of movies are chick flicks."

"I'm the guest, so I guess that means we watch my movie."

"First, then it'll be my turn."

"Deal."

She grabbed the remote and flipped on the disc player. The movie began to play the opening scenes as she settled in next to Jeremiah on the couch. Being here with him like this was surreal. She never thought this would ever happen to her. Sitting next to the guy she'd been in love with since tenth grade didn't happen to girls like her. *Well, they do now.*

"Are you enjoying the movie?" he asked as their hands brushed together in the midst of the popcorn bowl.

"Yeah. I like Bruce Willis."

"He's a pretty good actor."

"I'd say so. These action flicks are exciting."

"I thought you didn't like action flicks?"

"I never said that. I just said I figured you'd pick one rather than a chick flick. I happen to like movies with car crashes, shootings, and explosions." She turned to face him. "You know I almost went to school to be in stunts."

"Really?"

"Yep. I wanted to be one of those people who flew through the air and landed on one of those big airbags. It looked so fun when I visited Los Angeles and went to Universal Studios."

"Why didn't you?"

"Because Dad needed me here to take over the garage when he can't work on cars anymore. Being the only child sucks sometimes, but I love him."

"You have no idea how lost you get being part of a huge family like mine. Middle kid syndrome jumps on a lot of people when you have a family of nine kids."

"I can imagine it would be hard not to get lost in the shuffle, but you seem to do pretty well for yourself."

"It's even worse now with the extra women in the picture. Mom and Dad are all about the daughters-in-law and the grandkids these days."

"You make sure they're financially secure though, right? I mean, you are the reason they stay in business out there because you keep their finances straight."

"True, but it's not simple to stand out in the crowd gathering out there."

"Have you thought about getting married yourself?"

He laughed as he grabbed her hand. "Are you askin'?"

Her breath stopped in her throat. "Well no, but I wondered since you are getting close to thirty. Shouldn't it be about time?"

"You are too, you know. Are you feeling the itch to be married?"

"A little. My dad is hinting at marriage and grandkids although without a steady guy, it seems unlikely for the time being. With no boyfriend in the mix, it's hard to think about a future and a wedding, not to mention babies."

"We should just get married and put them all out of their misery."

She choked on the popcorn kernel in her mouth. "You can't be serious?"

"Of course not, silly. I'm kidding!"

"Oh, thank God! I mean, we don't really know each other. I could snore or something that you hate. I mean you were mad at me earlier for trying to be what you wanted, remember?" She took a breath to continue only to have him put his hand over her mouth.

"Easy girl. Lighten up, would you?" He tipped his head to the side as a grin spread across his lips. "I'm not about to get married to someone I don't know and am not hopelessly in love with, so calm down."

She blew out a forced exhale. "Good. Me either. I want to be madly in love with the man I marry someday."

"I hope you find him soon. You're a beautiful woman and being out there on the market can be hectic."

"You're teasing me now."

"Yes, I am. Stop being so serious. We're two friends having a nice evening watching a movie with popcorn." He held up a piece to feed her. "Nothing more."

For the next few hours, they joked, threw popcorn at each other and generally had a good time. It was something she'd needed. The stress of the garage, not having a dating life or a steady boyfriend had gotten to her.

"So what kind of girl *do* you like?"

"Well, let's see. Someone who is confident, real, likes kids, is close to her family, not so much into being the eye candy on my arm, but who likes to dress up once in a while and hit the town so every man in the room can't take his eyes off her."

He flipped off the movie since the credits were rolling at the end of *City of Angels.*

She dabbed at her eyes with a tissue from the box next to her on the table. That movie always made her cry. "Sorry."

"For what?"

"For blubbering. You probably didn't need to see me with traces of mascara running down my face."

He took the tissue from her hand as he turned her face toward his. She sucked in a breath as he gently wiped the smudge from beneath her eye. He was so close she could feel his breath on her lips. A shiver raced down her back when he stopped and looked down into her eyes. He leaned in like he planned to kiss her, or wanted to at least, and she closed her eyes in anticipation.

A bang in the hallway startled them both into a quick separation. "Sorry, kids."

"It's fine, Dad. Did you need something?"

"Just getting a glass of milk. Heartburn is killing me tonight."

"Are you sure you're okay?"

"I'm fine, honey. You two just keep doing what you were doing," he said with a wave of his hand.

The refrigerator door opened before the sounds of something being poured into a glass reached her on the couch. She glanced at Jeremiah who seemed to be contemplating something as he studied the picture on the wall above the fireplace with a hell of an intense look in his eyes. *What is he thinking? I feel really stupid now, hoping he would lean in and kiss me. It shouldn't be like that between us. We're friends. Nothing more, right? He doesn't want anything but friendship from me.* She wondered why he looked like he was going to kiss her then.

"I probably should get on home," Jeremiah said, climbing to his feet. "It was a great evening. We'll have to do it again sometime."

"How about tomorrow?"

"Tomorrow?"

"Yeah, are you busy?"

"No." He shoved his hand into his front pocket to retrieve his keys. "We could go to The Dusty Boot to shoot some pool or throw darts."

"Sounds like fun."

"Okay. I'll pick you up about seven unless you want to get some dinner beforehand. Maybe Aunt Anne's diner?"

"Sure. Sounds like fun."

"Great." He shuffled his feet for a second. "I guess I'll see you tomorrow then. Since we are doing dinner, I'll pick you up at six."

She got to her feet to walk him to his car. Dare she hope he would try to kiss her goodnight? A girl could always dream, right? "I'll walk you out."

As they walked to the door, she turned to glance at her father who stood holding up the kitchen island as if his life depended on it while he sipped his glass of milk with a smirk. *Jerk.* He knew how she felt about Jeremiah since she never kept anything from her dad.

The cooler night air hit her in the face as they walked outside toward Jeremiah's truck. "Thanks for tonight. It was a lot of fun even though things started rather badly." She rubbed her arms to ward off the chill.

"We discussed that. Be yourself. I like the Callie I know from the garage."

"Okay."

"I like the fancy dressed Callie too, but don't make yourself up to be something you aren't. I think you just like dressing up sometimes to be all girly."

"Sometimes. It's nice to be a woman occasionally."

"Tell you what, put on a pretty blouse or tank top tomorrow night with some jeans meant to show off your curves and you'll be just right."

She smiled at the thought of the perfect jeans for what she had in mind. "I can do that."

"Good. I'll be interested to see how your ass looks."

"You like my ass?"

"You have a very pretty one. Mind you, I'm an ass man."

"You don't say?"

"Yep. I love me some pretty, curvy butt in a nice, tight pair of jeans."

"I'll see what I can do then." The smile curving his lips made her want to kiss him all the more, but she figured it wasn't the right time.

"I'll see you tomorrow."

He leaned in and kissed her on the forehead. *Damn it! A little lower, please.*

"Thanks, Jeremiah."

He climbed into his truck, started the engine and pulled away from the curb.

She stood near the edge of the lawn, watching as he drove down her street. With a heavy sigh, she headed back into the house and her lonely bed.

"How'd things go?" her dad asked as she shut the front door behind her.

"Fine."

"Did he kiss you?"

"It's not like that between us, Daddy. He's just a friend and I think that's all he'll ever be to me. I want more, but he doesn't see me as girlfriend material."

"Well maybe you need to make him see you as the woman of his dreams."

"Maybe." She shrugged before she poured herself a glass of milk from the refrigerator as well. "I don't think we're very compatible on the romance level though."

"Why do you think so?"

Cold milk felt good on her throat, spreading through her chest. "I don't know. He doesn't act like he's interested in me as a girlfriend." She leaned against the counter, sipping on the white liquid in her glass as she contemplated exactly what to do about Jeremiah Young. Could she convince him she was everything he wanted and needed in a woman? She wasn't sure. Confidence wasn't one of her strong points, especially when she compared herself to the women in town like Lydia. "I'm not his type, Dad. He's always been seen with girly girls, not someone who works on cars."

Her father wrapped an arm around her shoulders, pulling her into a hug. "You have to understand one thing about men, Callie. They don't always know what they need until it slaps them in the face. There is a reason that boy hasn't settled down with a girly girl. Maybe he wants something different, like you."

"One can hope."

"Bide your time, sweetie. He'll come around."

Callie finished off her glass of milk, kissed her dad goodnight and headed to her room to try to sleep. She wasn't sure she'd be able to with the way tonight went or maybe she would dream of Jeremiah kissing her. That would be cool. Not like she didn't dream of him often anyway, at least now she knew the look in his eyes when he was about to kiss her, making the visual more potent.

Chapter Four

Jeremiah pulled up his chair in front of his desk at the ranch before he opened his desktop to his bank account. He pursed his lips as he nodded. He was almost there. Almost to the point where he could leave the ranch as a hand or financial advisor or whatever you wanted to call him. He'd made his first million two years ago. Now he was closing in on ten.

Birds chirped out the window of his office as he glanced outside. Fall in Bandera took on a burnished hue as the weather had started to turn cooler in the evenings, but the days could still be rather hot. For some reason, he felt the need to visit the barn, soak up the atmosphere, the smells, and the general cowboy way of life today. Maybe he'd talk to his brother Jeff for a bit. It seemed they hadn't talked in forever.

Jeff had his own life going with his girlfriend, Terri, and their kids. They seemed happy although he figured Jeff would have married her by now. Poor guy was so gun-shy over marriage he wouldn't do the deed and put a ring on the girl's finger. Terri seemed happy with the way things were, but Jeremiah figured deep down she wanted what every woman wanted, a happy marriage.

How did he feel about matrimony? He wanted a wife someday, someone to come home to, someone to help raise their children together. The picture of

Callinda Lewis popped into his head as he stared out the window. Why her? Why now? Surely he didn't feel anything besides friendship for her, although he had been about to kiss her the night before when her dad interrupted them. What would that kiss have been like? She said she wasn't a virgin, that kind of made him mad, but he didn't quite understand why. Maybe it was the fact that some kid had taken advantage of her in high school. He wouldn't have, would he?

Hard to say, he was all about getting laid back then, just like any other high schooler, but Callie was different. Good girls didn't do those kinds of things.

Had it been at prom for her? He thought about asking her. Maybe not. It really wasn't any of his business anyway. But who had she given her virginity to?

His had been some years before that. An older woman at the ranch had cornered him in the barn when he was sixteen. She'd been all about teaching him how to please her and boy did he ever! He used the skills she'd taught him over her two-week stay to learn all he could about making love to a woman. The women he'd been with since seemed to like his prowess. He smiled and then frowned. Could he take Callie to bed?

"What the hell? Why am I even thinking about getting her onto any old flat surface?"

Not that he didn't want a hot partner in the sack, but Callie? Well maybe. She sure looked gorgeous in that red dress she'd worn the night before. He pulled off his hat before wiping the sweat from his forehead. His jeans felt a bit tighter when he thought about how well she'd filled out that material. She was just a friend, right? He shouldn't be thinking about her all dirty like, but man, he'd wanted to kiss her when her dad interrupted. Her lips had looked so tempting, he'd almost lost himself in her mouth for a minute. Good thing her dad had stopped that nonsense. He couldn't afford to get tied up with a good girl. He'd always played the field and that's how he liked it, at least for now.

Later he would think about a wife, not now. He needed to get the family on an even keel with their money so they wouldn't have to worry for the long haul. His parents kept a pretty good eye on the bank account so he kept a different account for what investing he'd been doing. If they ever found out about him hiding their money, they'd kill him. He tapped a few keys on the keyboard, pulling up the account information for the ranch. He'd been investing pretty heavily for them for the last year. The sum had a few more zeros than there had been when he'd started. He was proud to say the ranch now had at least enough to cover them for awhile should things go south.

His mom stopped in the doorway to his office just as he clicked off the page. "Jeremiah?"

"Hi, Mom."

"What are you up to this morning? You don't usually work on the weekends."

"Not computer work anyway. I was checking on things from the stock's closing yesterday to see where things were."

"You've become quite the financial wizard, son."

He smiled as his mom put her hand on his shoulder to peek over at the computer screen. "Yeah. Things are going well."

"When are you going to let your dad and me in on the buying and selling of stock so we can invest for our retirement?"

"Soon."

"Good. I'd like to sit down with you to talk numbers. You know I have a degree in mathematics."

"I know. It's probably where I got my love of numbers."

She leaned in to kiss him on the cheek. "Probably." She turned to go out of the office, but stopped for a second. "Oh, how was your date with Callinda Lewis last night?"

"It wasn't really a date, Mom. We were just hanging out as friends."

"You know you could do a lot worse than her. She's a nice girl."

"I know."

"You should think about her on the girlfriend level. She'd be good for you. Nice, down-to-earth kind of girl to go with my wild son."

"I'm not wild. I'm tame compared to some of my brothers."

"True, but you aren't the settling down forever kind of cowboy right now and I think you should be."

"Why? I'm not that old yet."

"You're getting there, son. Just like your brothers, you don't want to think about being with one woman. I've heard about your escapades with the women of Bandera and San Antonio. I think you need to find a nice girl. I think Callinda Lewis is just what you need." She pressed her palm to his cheek before she turned back toward the door to leave. "Think about it."

Great. That's all I need is to have Mom on the Callie Lewis bandwagon. Once she sets her mind on someone for one of her sons, there's no stopping her meddling.

He didn't need to think about it since he'd already been doing a lot of it about that particular woman since last night. *Damn it!* He was a forever kind of guy, right?

With a flick of the switch, he turned off the monitor on his computer. He climbed to his feet as he scraped his fingers over the stubble on his chin. He'd have to shower and shave for his date with Callie.

Shit. Even he was thinking of their meeting tonight as a date when he shouldn't be. He didn't need the complication of a permanent woman in his life until he was ready to move on from being a cowboy. He might get there sometime, but he sure wasn't ready yet.

It was still early in the day. Not yet noon. He might just take a group of riders out on the next excursion, just for the hell of it. He hadn't done a ride along in forever it seemed. He might be out of practice a bit, but being a cowboy since he could walk, the whole thing came naturally to him. You get right back on when you fall off.

Lunch would be served soon so he'd get with Jeff then so they could talk business with his dad too. He needed to get their take on the expenses for the coming month before the guest population died off at the end of September. After Labor Day, things were slower around the ranch for guests, but the cattle business never took a break.

He adjusted his hat on his head to settle it low on his brow as he glanced down at his work clothes. Dusty boots, Wrangler jeans, standard cowboy hat and western style shirt. He sure looked the part anyway. With a wiry twist of his lips and a shrug, he walked out before shutting the door behind him. Not that anyone would mess with his computer, but he didn't want to take the chance. He wasn't ready to reveal just how well things were going with his own finances, much less the ranch.

The lunch bell clanged in the distance, signaling food was served although the guests ate first and then the family. The ranch had a few empty beds the last week or so, but there were still several people hanging out for those last few days of summer before things wound down. He knew of a few single ladies who were checking out the cowboys on the ranch this week. They'd given him the eye yesterday before supper. He knew his mom's rule of getting together with the guests, but he wondered if it might be a good idea to check out one. He had an itch that hadn't been scratched lately.

What about Callie?

There she was in the forefront of his mind again. He didn't need to think of her when he thought of bedding a lady, but there she was making herself a present part of his thoughts without regard to the fact that he wanted to keep things strictly friends with her. Did he? His thoughts strayed to how she'd looked in her slinky little red dress last night, bringing randy images of her to the front of his brain. Maybe she would be interested in taking their relationship to a friends with benefits status?

Hmm.

When he rounded the corner of the stairs to walk into the dining room, he was struck by the group of people milling about. With a family of nine boys, his own group made up a large portion of the people in the room and with the addition of some of the boys and their significant others, made for an even bigger group.

The single women he'd been eyeing yesterday had already sat down to eat at the back end of the dining room tables. "Jeremiah? Come sit with us."

He tipped his hat before he got in line to get his plate. Nothing like a little female company to make the hours go by faster.

Once he got his plate of food, he stopped by the family table to tell Jeff he needed to talk to him after lunch before he headed toward the ladies at the back of the room. "Ladies."

A petite brunette scooted to one side. "Sit by me."

He took the seat and laid his hat on the bench between them. "Are you ladies having a good time?" The woman next to him, what was her name. Oh yeah, Brenda. "How about you, Brenda?"

"Well, yes. I mean there are all kinds of things to do on a place this size, but we wanted to get to know the cowboys *a lot* better than we have, if you know what I mean." She squeezed his thigh as she batted her eyelashes at him.

He glanced over at her, raising his eyebrow in question. Nope, he wasn't mistaken. Desire was written all over her face. He might take her up on that offer after a ride this afternoon. Maybe he'd take her for a private little outing down by the creek where two people could get to know each other a little bit. "How would you like to go for a ride with me this evening?"

"I would love to."

"I'll meet you here about six. After supper."

She smiled as her friends gasped and sighed. They finished lunch with the conversation floating around him of typical female proportions. He couldn't keep it all straight since he wasn't up on the latest fashions in New York, Broadway musicals, what the celebs were doing in Los Angeles, or even what the latest weather forecast was if it wasn't for their area. Yeah, he kept up on financial news, but women didn't care about that sort of thing.

When he finished his meal, he excused himself with work to be done never ending on a ranch and left the ladies to gossip amongst themselves.

He dumped his plate into the wash basin for the dishes with a smile toward Mandy who had just come out to grab the dirty plates. "What are your plans for tonight, Jeremiah?"

"Oh, I have a late night ride with a lady who is a guest here. I'm supposed to meet her at seven."

"That'll be great. I'm sure she'll enjoy your company."

Mandy grabbed the dishpan right before she disappeared through the double doors leading to the kitchen.

He pulled off his hat and rake his fingers through his hair. Why did he get the feeling he was forgetting something? He shrugged. Apparently, it wasn't important.

His mom walked up behind him as Mandy left through the doors. "I thought you were going out with Callie tonight?"

"Shit. I'd forgotten about that."

"Well you can't be in two places at once."

"No. I'll cancel with Callie."

"Why?"

"It'll be better that way. I don't want her to get the wrong idea, Mom. Two dates in two days? If she thinks there is something going to happen between us, she's mistaken."

"Jeremiah, you are being an ass."

"Sorry, but this is for the best."

"You're going out with a guest on the ranch?"

"Just going for a late evening ride."

"Uh-huh."

"Nothing else."

"Don't forget to call Callie. You'll really be in hot water if you do."

The family had finished up their food as well so he motioned for Jeff and his dad to join him in his office to go over the figures for the month on the supplies.

* * * *

Callie finished dressing in her tight-fitting jeans, white tank top with a sheer blouse she wanted to wear over the top lying on the bed, and her cowboy boots. She planned to be the epitome of what Jeremiah wanted in a woman if it killed her. With a glance at the clock, she realized he should be here any minute so she finished with the light bit of makeup before she clipped her hair back in a barrette. Nothing like being the girl next door and still trying to be a woman a cowboy would be interested in dating on a regular basis. "What if he kisses me tonight?" She closed her eyes as she imagined the look he had on his face when he bent his head to kiss her. He'd been about to, she just knew it, and man did she want him to.

"Callie?"

"Yeah, Dad?"

"Are you about ready? Jeremiah should be here any time."

"Yes. I'll be out in a minute if he comes to the door. I need to put on my blouse."

"All right. I'll man the door."

Fifteen minutes later, she paced in front of the fireplace as she glanced at her watch. Six-fifteen. She'd never known Jeremiah to be late for anything. Maybe she should call him. She had his number from when he'd tutored her so many years ago. She'd never erased it from her phone, always hoping someday he would call her. Well, now he should have and hadn't.

"Why don't you call him? Maybe something happened. He might have forgotten or he got in an accident or whatever."

"I should, huh?"

"Yes, you should."

"Okay." She exhaled forcibly, picked up her phone from the coffee table and scrolled through the numbers to find his. When she had his name highlighted, she hit talk so it would dial his number.

The phone rang several times before it he finally picked up with a breathless hello.

"Jeremiah?"

"Callie?"

"Uh, I thought I'd check with you since you're late. I thought you said six?"

"Oh, shit. God."

A female voice in the background said, "Hey, baby. Where are you going? We're just getting started, cowboy."

"Callie, I'm sorry. I was going to call you. Something came up and…"

"Something came up? Why do I hear a woman in the background?"

"She's a guest at the ranch."

"And the water in the background too?"

"She's in the restroom."

"Why don't I believe you, Jeremiah? If you didn't want to go out tonight, you could have at least called me."

"I meant to."

"You meant to cancel our date because you wanted to go out with a guest at the ranch?"

"Yes, I mean no. Shit."

"Never mind. I understand. I'll talk to you some other time."

"Callie?"

"What?"

"I'm sorry. I'll make it up to you. I promise."

"Fuck you, Jeremiah Young. Do your guest. Get your fucking rocks off because you aren't worth my time, you asshole." Too bad they didn't have a land line. It just wasn't the same forcibly hitting end on a cell phone.

Tears rolled down her cheeks. She should have known. All men were the same. They didn't give a shit about how things were supposed to work. He was supposed to be different. He was supposed to care about her even a little bit, but he didn't apparently. He was more interested in doing one of the guests at the ranch. *Fucker.*

"Aw, baby, I'm sorry."

She hiccupped as she pressed her fist to her mouth and bit down to try to relieve some of the pain she felt. "He's with someone at the ranch, Daddy. He couldn't even take the time to call me and cancel before he took off for parts unknown with some sleazeball guest who wants to fuck a cowboy."

"I know, honey. He's not worth your tears if he's that kind of man."

"God help me."

"It's okay. You should go out tonight anyway. Find yourself a nice young man to hang out with at the bar. Get a little crazy."

She wiped the tears from her face with a tissue from the coffee table. "I think I will, Daddy. Who knows? Maybe I'll meet the man of my dreams, the one who will take the place of Jeremiah Young and shred the thoughts of him right from my mind with one smile."

"I hope so, baby."

"I'm going to touch up my makeup before I head over to The Dusty Boot."

"You do that."

She hugged her dad, and then headed back down the hall to her bedroom to fix her face. When she glanced in the mirror of her bathroom, she saw the red rimmed eyes and blotchy face staring back. "He's not worth the tears. Asshole. I can't believe he did that." A fresh tear slid down her cheek, but she wiped it away angrily. "He's not worth my tears. I thought he was different. Apparently not. If it means a piece of ass, he's all about the most readily available women around. Well, to hell with him. He could have gotten it from me, but no. Asshole wanted some chick on the ranch. Probably a blonde bimbo with big boobs or something." She wiped the mascara that had bled under her eyes so she could refresh the look she'd perfected before.

She'd teach him and his wandering ways. She'd find herself a cowboy to fuck for the night so she could totally forget all about Jeremiah Young. If she was lucky, she might run into her forever cowboy and it wouldn't be him.

Several minutes later, she found herself standing at the open doorway of The Dusty Boot. Music blared through the speakers next to the band playing country music with a two-step beat to it. She wanted a drink. Something strong. Whiskey and Coke maybe.

She found an empty stool at the bar between two men she didn't know. Right up her alley.

Peyton Young made her way toward her to take her drink order and she had to bite her lip to keep from saying something about Jeremiah to his sister-in-law. Of course, it wasn't her fault or Jason's Jeremiah turned out to be an ass. "Hi there." She tilted her head to the side and smiled. "Callie, isn't it?"

"Yes. Hi, Peyton."

"What'll ya have, doll?"

"Jack and Coke, please."

"Coming right up."

As Peyton mixed the drink for her not far from where she sat, she glanced to her left to take in the man next to her. Nope, not her type. Older guy with a beer gut, large belt buckle and cowboy hat probably covering a half-bald head. She looked to her right. Now there was a possibility. The guy sitting next to her was cute. Dark hair peeked out beneath a straw cowboy hat, western style button-down shirt, nice jeans and dirty boots. He apparently worked for a living if he wore dirty boots to the bar.

"Hey."

He looked her way as he brought the beer bottle to his lips. When he finished the sip, he said, "Hi, pretty lady."

She blushed at the compliment as she held out her hand. "My name is Callie."

He took her hand. "Nice to meet you, Callie. I'm Matt."

"Do you live around here? I don't remember seeing you before."

"Nope. Live in San Antonio, but I heard this was a great bar to come to on Saturday night so here I am." He turned to check out the dance floor. "Seems to be a great place."

"Yeah."

"You live around here?"

"Yeah. My dad owns the garage up the road."

"Cool."

He tapped his foot to the beat of the music coming from the band as Peyton slid her drink to her on a napkin. "Six-fifty."

"Can I run a tab? I think I might be drinking a bit tonight."

"Sure. Just give me your card and I'll run it."

"Thanks."

She sipped the drink a let out a small cough.

"Strong?" he asked, one eyebrow shot up over his left eye.

"Yeah, a little. I'm not quite used to it being that strong, I guess."

"They make some pretty mean drinks here, I heard."

"They are pretty generous with the booze, that's for sure."

"Hey, want to dance?"

"Let me finish this drink first and I'd love to."

"How old are you, Callie?"

"Twenty-eight. Why?"

"Just checkin'. You look young, but the bartender didn't card you so I figured you were over twenty-one anyway."

"I know her. She knows me. In fact, most everyone in this bar probably knows me." She looked around the room noting several people she'd went to high school with, a group of the single Young brothers in the corner playing pool, another group of women she knew from around town and there was Lydia hanging all over a good-looking cowboy who worked on one of the other ranches in the area. Boy, she didn't take long finding another hunk. "Yep. I know most everyone in here."

"Maybe I should have you introduce me around. I could use some work."

"Are you a cowboy?"

He tipped his hat. "As cowboy as they come. Been wranglin' for a while now, but the ranch I've been working on sold out recently to a big conglomerate so they won't be running cattle anymore."

"I'm sorry."

"What do you do?"

"I work at my dad's garage."

"Oh, like running the cash register or something?"

"No, I'm a mechanic."

"Really. You work on cars, huh? Not a typical job for a woman."

"No, it's not, but I enjoy doing it and since I'm my dad's only child, I got to learn his trade." She set her empty glass on the bar. "Shall we dance now?"

"Sure."

He took her hand in his and led her to the dance floor. His touch didn't do what Jeremiah's did. She didn't tingle or shiver from the brush of his fingers. She hoped she could get past that because she really did want to like this guy. However, when he wrapped a hand behind her head, he almost punched him. She didn't like being manhandled.

She took his hand and put it on her waist.

"Sorry."

"No problem. I don't like a guy's hand up there is all. It's more comfortable on my waist."

"Okay."

They danced a two-step while she kept looking around the bar. Her vision caught on the other Young brothers playing pool in the corner and her thoughts strayed to Jeremiah. What was he doing? Was he doing the guest from the ranch? Where were they? She'd heard water running in the background, but that could've meant anything. Jeremiah shared half of one of the cabins with one of his brothers, but he could have taken her there. They might have been sharing a bath when he answered the phone or maybe in her room?

"Bastard."

"Excuse me?"

"Sorry. I didn't mean you. I was thinking about someone else."

He placed his hand on his chest. "Ouch. You're dancing with me and thinking about another guy?"

"I'm sorry. I didn't mean to insult you."

"Did you have a fight with your boyfriend tonight? Is that why you're at the bar prowling?"

"I'm not prowling. You make it sound like I'm some slut looking to get laid because my boyfriend cheated on me." They stopped dancing as she jammed her hands on her hips. "I'll have you know I don't have a boyfriend and we didn't have a fight. I'm not here looking to get laid, I'm just here to have a few drinks and unwind, so you can kiss my ass, Matt." She spun on her heel to head back for the bar to get another drink. Strike one.

"Wait a damned minute here. You're the one who muttered bastard I'm asking what's the issue here. I need to know where I stand because it's Saturday and I don't want to go home alone."

"Well if you're looking to get laid, find another girl. I know of several here who are into that kind of thing."

"And you aren't?"

She pulled back her hand and slapped him hard across the cheek. "No, I'm not. Get lost before I deck your ass."

He grabbed her hand and pulled her in, squashing her breasts against his chest. "Like it rough, do you?"

"The lady said get lost, buddy."

Without glancing over Matt's shoulder, she knew who stood a few feet away. Jeremiah.

"Find your own. This one is mine."

"She said no, now let her go before I haul your ass outside for the beating you deserve for manhandling a lady."

Matt pushed her back and raised his hands. "No harm done."

She finally glanced behind Matt to meet Jeremiah's gaze. He looked furious. Well, to hell with him. She had every right to be pissed at him, not him with her. She hadn't done anything wrong. "Jeremiah."

"Callie," he said, his voice turning soft.

Don't fall for it. He's not worth it. He can grovel all he wants, but he was the one who couldn't even take the time out to call you and cancel your date before he went off to fuck some cowboy groupie from the ranch.

"I'm sorry."

"You're sorry? You should be."

He held out his hand. She almost reached for him, but kept her arms across her chest where she'd folded them the minute Matt let her go.

"Let me make it up to you."

"How do you propose to do that, Jeremiah? I'm not falling for your cowboy charm, good looks, and easy way with women. You couldn't even take the time to call me—"

The band started playing again cutting off her words so she couldn't even hear herself think.

"Let's go outside," he said next to her ear so she could hear him. The sensation of his breath on her neck drove her crazy. Goose bumps broke out on her skin, zipping down and back up to settle right between her legs.

"Damn him."

"What?"

"Nothing. Fine. Let's go outside."

He placed his hand at the small of her back as he led her out through the front door into the cooler night air. "My truck is over there."

With a roll of her eyes, she walked toward the big silver dually sitting to the left of the doors. She wasn't going to let him off so easy. He'd hurt her even if there wasn't anything between them except friendship. Standing her up without even a phone call was inexcusable in her book.

"What can I do, Callie?"

"Nothing."

"There has to be something, darlin'."

She stomped her foot. Yeah, it made her look like a five-year-old, but it let off some of the anger she'd been holding in since he interrupted her exchange with Matt. "Don't you darlin' me, mister. I'm so pissed at you right now I could punch you."

"I screwed up. I know that now."

"Now? It didn't cross your mind when you made the date with the chick from the ranch that you had already made a date with me."

"Ours wasn't a date. We were going out as friends."

"Whatever, Jeremiah. I considered it a date whether it was between a guy and his girl or two friends. You fucked up."

"I know." He rubbed his hand up and down her arm. "I realize I shouldn't have even made the date with the other girl since I already had plans with you."

"Why did you?"

"She was available." He shrugged. "I haven't gotten laid in months." He raked his fingers through his hair before putting his hat back on his head. "I don't know, Callie."

"I didn't even cross your mind when you made the date with her, huh?"

"At first no. I remembered after she'd already left. I promise, I planned to call you and cancel, but it slipped my mind."

"So you would have rather went out with her than me."

"I was guaranteed to get laid with her. I wasn't with you."

"I told you last night I would be up for a one-night stand."

"True, but it felt like I would be using you."

"If sex is what you want, Jeremiah, I'm game, but I won't be used. I'm worth more than that. Every woman is worth more than that even if they don't think so. Men aren't on this planet to get laid every time their dick twitches, but they sure as hell think so. As for me, you can find someone else to hang out with, do the dirty deed with or whatever. My value is too high for your bank account, baby. You don't have enough money to buy me."

His lips twitched with a grin he couldn't hide. She wanted to smack him.

"I said I'm sorry. What more can I do to make it up to you?"

"You know what, there isn't anything you can do. I'm so over you, it's not funny. I'm tired of wanting you. I'm tired of loving you from afar. I'm done." She spun on her heels to head back into the bar, but before she got too far, he grabbed her arm and spun her around.

"What did you say?"

She jerked her arm out of his hold. "Nothing. Fuck off." Without a backward glance, she yanked open the door on the bar and strolled back inside. She planned to get really drunk so she could forget all about Jeremiah Young.

* * * *

"That girl is going to get herself into trouble in there with the rowdy bunch here tonight." Jeremiah shook his head as he followed Callie back into the bar. *I'll just stay to keep an eye on her so she doesn't do something stupid like go home with one of those cowboys.* He headed for a corner booth and slid in behind the table. The waitress rolled her hips in a come-and-get-me fashion as she walked up to his table to take his order. "Beer, please."

"Coming right up, Jeremiah." She leaned in close. "I get off at ten if you want to hook up."

"No thanks."

She straightened up and huffed loudly as she spun on her heels to head back to the bar.

Callie rapped her knuckles on the mahogany to get Peyton's attention. "Peyton, give me a shot of tequila and a Corona."

"Shit. She's drinkin' hard from the get-go. I'd better watch her closely." He moved in close so he could keep a good eye on her, but also so he could hear what they were saying. Callie couldn't see him sitting close from where he took up a spot a few stools down from her.

Peyton's eyebrow shot up. "Patrón?"

"That'll do."

"Coming right up."

Peyton moved down the bar and leaned in toward her friend Mandy. "Hey, keep an eye on her, would you? Make friends. She could use one, I think."

"Sure," Mandy replied, grabbing her beer and moving closer. "Hey. I'm Mandy. I'm a good friend of Peyton's. You look like you could use a friend."

"If you want to get stinking drunk with me, then I'll be your best buddy."

"Sounds like a plan to me. I hate drinking alone."

"Name's Callie."

"Nice to meet you. Who are you trying to forget tonight?"

"One of those pain in the ass Young brothers."

Jeremiah's heart thumped in his chest. Was she trying to forget him? He hoped she wasn't so tied up in him he'd hurt her. He didn't want to do that to her.

"Sounds like you and I will be best friends. I could get used to forgetting one myself."

Peyton slid the drink toward her. "I'm shooting tequila. You with me?"

"You got it, babe." Mandy nodded for Peyton to hand her one too as Callie waited for her so they could down the potent liquid together.

The minute they both had a shot glass in their hands, they sprinkled salt on the back of their fist, downed the shot with toss of their heads, quickly bit into the lime wedge on the Corona bottle, then downed a swallow of the beer. "Oh my God, that's nasty."

"You going again?"

"Hell yeah!" Mandy's eyes narrowed as she glanced behind Callie and locked gazes with him.

He wondered which of his brothers she wanted to forget. Obviously she had it bad for one of them and wasn't getting the attention she wanted. Mandy seemed like a nice girl from what he knew about her. Maybe he could help her out a little if he knew which brother caught her interest. Right now he had to keep an eye on Callie though. At the rate she was going, she'd be shit-faced inside of fifteen minutes.

For the next few hours, he watched her closely as she downed shot after shot of tequila with the Corona shooter. The two women got giggly, laughing at everything. She was kind of cute when she got like this, he had to admit.

Then she started inviting men to do body shots. He growled low in his throat at each one in turn as they approached. They didn't heed his warning look and there wasn't much he could do really. She wasn't his girlfriend. At this point she wasn't even his friend according to her, but he still watched out for her.

The men would lick the salt off her neck and then shoot the tequila. His stomach knotted with each jerk who took a shot at her.

Unable to take anymore, he finally grabbed her arm and turned her to face him. "What the hell do you think you're doing? These men are all over you."

She just shot back with, "This is my party and I'll do body shots if I want to. You didn't want what I offered, well maybe one of these other guys does."

He didn't reply to her shot across the bow. She was pretty drunk and it wouldn't do much good to argue with her. *Damn her.* Lusting after her wasn't the hard part, realizing she wanted him too was difficult for him to fathom. She'd been a friend for so long, it was hard for him to think of her beyond friendship, but lately he definitely wanted more from her. Friends with benefits, maybe. He could do something along those lines without a problem.

For now, he would sit back in the corner he'd taken up residence in after she'd told him off, and glower at anyone who got too friendly with her. She wasn't going to let him get between her and her little pity party or whatever it was. She didn't want him around so he'd watch her from afar making sure she didn't get into too much trouble. Yeah, he'd screwed up by forgetting to call her, but the really screwed up part was after he'd gone out riding with the guest from the ranch, he didn't want to be with the woman anymore. When she'd basically thrown herself at him while they'd stopped to water the horses at the pool, he'd had to practically push her off him. All he could think about was Callie, especially after her phone call. How messed up was it to want to be with her when he had a perfectly willing woman right there?

As soon as Callie had hung up, he'd taken the woman back to the ranch, stabled the horses and drove into town. He had a feeling she would go out without him to The Dusty Boot. Sure enough, he'd found her not long after he'd arrived. He'd tried to talk some sense into her and get her to forgive him, but no. Stupid girl. Didn't she know he'd do anything for her?

Chapter Five

Sunlight poured through the curtains of her bedroom, blinding her with its intensity and making her head feel like it wanted to split wide open. "Oh God. What the hell did I do last night?"

At least I'm not waking up in a strange motel room with something worse like a guy I don't know or maybe even worse, a guy I do know…unless it happened to be Jeremiah. I would hope to have remembered sleeping with him.

Her mouth felt like cotton dried up every bit of saliva she had. She remembered shooting tequila with some women she knew from town who seemed to be hell-bent on forgetting a man or two. Peyton's friend Mandy had been there. They'd become fast friends over several shots of tequila. It seemed they both wanted to forget a Young brother. Mandy had her sights set on one of them and kept getting the cold shoulder. Callie, well she knew what hell she was going through without regard to Jeremiah. *The asshole.*

Rolling over, she let a moan escape as her stomach revolted against the movement. She jumped up from her bed and rushed for the bathroom only to hug the toilet as dry heaves wracked her body. *Jesus, please let me die right here. I promise, I'll be good in heaven. I can't handle this.*

Her cell phone jingled on her nightstand in the other room, but there was no way in hell she would be able to answer it hugging the commode.

Her father grabbed the phone. "Hello? Oh hi, Jeremiah. No, she's not up to talking right now."

"I don't want to talk to that asshole. Tell him to bug off."

"She's hugging the toilet at the moment."

"Fuck him!" She heaved again, coughing like her lungs would burst from her chest. They burned like they were on fire as her stomach rebelled against any thoughts of contents.

"I'll tell her to call you when she's feeling better."

"I'm not calling him. He can go to hell."

"All right. Talk to you later then. Bye."

"Why didn't you tell him to go to hell?"

"Because we don't talk like that in this house, especially on Sunday."

"Sorry, but he deserves it."

Her father placed a cool washcloth on her head. "I'm sure he does."

"Oh lordy, that feels like heaven."

"How did you get home? Your car isn't in the drive."

"I took a cab, I guess."

"Got a bit drunk?"

"Yeah, just a little. Mandy is my new best friend."

"Mandy?"

"Yeah, she's a friend of the bartender who is married to one of the Young boys. Mandy is her friend, but she's my new best friend too. We were doing shots of tequila."

"Oh, boy."

"With beer shooters."

"No wonder you're sick. I'll get you some Alka-Seltzer. I'm sure I have some in my bathroom."

"I love you, Dad."

"I'm sure you do, honey. I've been where you are a few times in my life so I know what it feels like to be hung over." Her dad disappeared out the door, but was back in a few minutes with a glass of water with something fizzing in it. "This will either cure what ails you or make you throw up."

"I'm already throwing up."

"It'll help calm your stomach, sweetie. Trust me."

With a dubious glance at her father, she took the glass and sipped at the fizzling liquid.

"Shoot it."

She made a face, plugged her nose and swallowed the entire glass in a matter of a few gulps. "Good God, that's nasty." Her stomach heaved a few times, but nothing came up as she rested her forehead on the cool porcelain. She'd never leave the bathroom again.

Her father took her hand to bring her to her feet. "Now up you go."

"I can't."

"Sure you can. You need some ibuprofen and a few more hours of sleep. You'll be good as new." He helped her to her feet and slowly walked her to her bed. "Lie down."

Once he placed the cool cloth over her eyes and she'd taken the ibuprofen, he told her to sleep. He'd hold off the hoards of admirers until she felt better. She wasn't sure what the hell he meant, but right now she didn't care. Her head hurt, her stomach felt a little better for now, and she wanted to close her gritty eyelids to rest. A little sleep would do her wonders.

Several hours later, she groaned as she rolled over in her bed to the chirping of her cell phone indicating she had a text message. When she picked up the phone so she could press the button, her eyes widened to see twenty-five messages that weren't all from the same guy. "What the hell?"

"Apparently you were pretty free last night with your phone number and address. I've had at least ten men here today wanting to talk to you while you slept. Your phone has been chirping like a bird in heat for the last few hours."

"Shit."

"Callinda."

"Sorry, Dad. I wish I could remember what I did."

"You might ask Peyton since she was probably one of the few people there who weren't drunk last night."

"But that would mean going out to the Young ranch. I don't have her number."

"I still think you should find out before your popularity gets my lawn messed up with the cars and trucks going across it."

"Maybe Mandy will remember. I think I have her number." She pushed her hand into her jeans pocket only to come out with a wad of papers. "What the heck is this?" She spread them on her bed before opening one to find a guy's name and number. "Holy crap!" She opened two more. "These are all phone numbers."

"You've become one very popular young lady."

"I need to call Mandy." She grabbed her cell phone off the nightstand and flipped through the numbers until she found what she was looking for. After she pushed the button to call Mandy, she waited until her new friend picked up with a groggy reply. "Mandy?"

"Yeah. Who is this?"

"Callie."

"Oh, hey, sister in crime. How are you feeling today?"

"Better right now after my dad plied me with home remedies for hangovers, but I still need to get some food in my stomach."

"Don't mention food. I'm so sick my eyes are crossed."

"Listen, I need you to tell me what the heck happened last night."

"Why? You don't remember?"

"No. My phone is about to blow up from text messages, my dad said there have been at least ten guys at my door today, and I have a pocket full of phone numbers."

"I tell you what, let me rouse myself out of bed to get a shower. I'll meet you at Anne's diner for some coffee and food. We'll talk, because honey, you need to be better prepared. You made a lot of friends last night."

"Crap. Okay. I'll meet you there in half an hour."

"Sounds good. See you in a few. Oh, and you're gonna love what you said to Jeremiah when he tried to break up your little party."

With a swipe of the button, she hung up with Mandy as she tipped her head back on her shoulders, wondering what kind of mess she'd gotten herself into this time.

When she walked into the diner a half an hour later, she kept her sunglasses on and took a table in the back. She didn't want anyone to see her in case she was recognized from her escapades at The Dusty Boot last night.

Anne moved to her table and asked, "Coffee?"

"Definitely, two cups. I'm meeting someone in a few minutes. I think she'll want some too."

"Callinda?"

"Shh." She put up her hand to shush Anne. "I don't want anyone to see me."

"Why? You usually come in here every Sunday with your dad anyway. Most people would expect you to be here." She tapped her fingernail on the table. "Where is your father, by the way?" She tilted her head to the side. "And why are you wearing those dark glasses?"

"I'm hung over. My head is beginning to pound again so please keep your voice down."

"Hung over from what? Did you party too hard?"

"You could say that."

Mandy came through the door and Callie waved her over to the booth she'd secured.

"The two of you must have really got into trouble last night," Anne said as she poured the second cup of coffee for Mandy.

"You are a saint, Anne."

"Just being me."

Mandy sipped the strong brew while she cradled the cup between her hands. "Thank you, God. You have no idea how much I needed this."

"I've been there a few times myself, girls. I know how it feels. What you need is some breakfast."

"But you don't serve breakfast this late in the day," Mandy said.

"I'll whip something up for you two. Be right back."

"She's such a great lady." Mandy sipped the coffee again before she braced her elbows on the table. "So, what do you remember?"

"Not a damned thing."

"From what point on?"

She slowly lowered her sunglasses, then laid them on the table. "Not much after my argument with Jeremiah outside."

"He watched you all night, you know."

"He did?"

Mandy nodded, sipping the coffee. "He sat in the corner, but kept an eagle eye on you even though you had every single man watching you. You were dancing on top of the bar."

"Oh, hell."

"Yes, ma'am. You took off that clingy little blouse you had on and tucked your tank top into your bra. When the guys started lining up to do belly shots off you, he growled."

"Growled?"

"Yep, but it didn't stop the guys from licking the salt from your neck before they took the shots. You even let one guy do one from between your boobs."

"Oh, God. I'm so screwed."

"Honey, you are one of the most popular women in this town right now. You shouldn't have any problems getting a date for a long time to come."

She pushed her hair off her forehead. "But Mandy, that's not me. It was the alcohol."

"Live it up while you've got it, babe. Jeremiah can wait."

"You said something about me telling him off when he tried to stop my party?"

"Oh, yeah." Mandy laughed before she groaned as she rubbed her temples for a second. "God, my head is killing me."

Callie laid a hand on Mandy's arm. "Alka-Seltzer and ibuprofen. Does wonders."

The look Mandy gave her said she wished she could curl into a ball and just die. "Your dad's recipe?"

"Worked for me. I feel okay now. Not perfect, but okay." Callie tapped her fingernail on the table. "So spill. Tell me what I said to Jeremiah."

"What's going on with you two anyway?"

"Nothing."

With her head tilted to the side like she didn't believe her, Mandy said, "Nothing my ass. The man doesn't growl, for God's sake, when some guy wants to do body shots from between your boobs without a reason."

Callie smiled. *Jeremiah growled?* "So tell me. What did I say?"

"You said, 'This is my party and I'll do body shots if I want to. You didn't want what I offered, well maybe one of these other guys does.'"

"What did he say?"

"He didn't say anything, just moved back to his corner and watched you for the rest of the night, although he did make sure you got home. I'm pretty sure he drove you there himself. The last I saw you, he was putting you in the front of his truck. Since you made it home okay, I assume he took you there."

"He took me home?"

"Yeah. You were waving to all the other men who saw you outside, but he was the one who poured you into his vehicle to make sure you got home all right and didn't get taken advantage of in your drunken state."

Anne brought two plates heaping with scrambled eggs, bacon, hash browns and toast to their table. "Eat up, girls."

"Oh, Lord. I don't think I can eat this greasy food," Mandy replied, holding her hand over her mouth.

"Here are two ibuprofen and some Alka-Seltzer for your stomach."

"What's with you old people and your remedies? That's what my dad gave me this morning."

"It works, don't it?"

"Yes, ma'am."

"Then hush." She handed Mandy the glass. "Drink up. Quickly. You'll feel better in about five minutes. You need to eat."

"Okay." Mandy downed the entire glass, shuddering with the last gulp. "Oh, my God. That's nasty shit."

"Yeah, but you'll feel better."

"I hope so. I hate hangovers."

"I've never had one before, but I didn't care for mine either," Callie replied. "I hit the toilet first thing this morning as soon as I opened my eyes."

"Your phone call woke me up from mine."

Callie took Mandy's hand to squeeze her fingers in shared misery. "Sorry."

A small smile spread across Mandy's lips. "It was totally worth it. I actually got a few phone numbers myself."

Callie started eating the food in front of her, talking in between bites. "So tell me what else Jeremiah did."

"Not much of anything. He glowered most of the night as he watched you spreading yourself kind of thin around the men in the bar. You had them hanging all over you, especially when you were doing body shots. He didn't like seeing you doing that at all was my guess."

"Well, tough shit."

"My thoughts exactly." Mandy sipped at her coffee, simply sighing after she swallowed. "I love coffee and I actually think I might be able to eat some of this food now." After a couple of tentative bites, she started eating with gusto. "This is really good."

"I need my jolt of java every morning before I go to the station, otherwise I'm a bear."

"So, tell me what's the deal with you two anyway?"

"Nothing much. We were friends, or so I thought. You know, acquaintances or whatever you want to call it. He asked me out Friday."

"Like a date?"

"I'm not sure what the hell it was. We went out to dinner, then went back to my house and watched movies. It wasn't a big deal, but he did ask if I wanted to go out Saturday too after I suggested another date, to hang out at the bar, play pool. That kind of thing. He stood me up for some guest at the ranch who wanted to ride a cowboy. I told him off before he apparently showed up at the bar when I came alone. You know the rest better than I do."

"He acted jealous last night."

"Jealous? Not in this lifetime. He doesn't care about me other than being friends."

"I don't know. The way things went down last night sure doesn't make me think he doesn't care."

"Well, he doesn't. If he did, he wouldn't have stood me up in the first place."

"Maybe he's scared? I know how those Young boys tend to run from feelings too deep. Just asked Peyton, Paige, Mesa, and Terri."

"Scared? I doubt it. I don't think anything frightens Jeremiah. He's tough as nails."

Mandy finished her food and pushed her plate away. "Except when it comes to women, especially one he cares about more than he wants to admit."

"Enough about me and Jeremiah. Who are you trying to forget?"

"Jonathan."

"Why?"

"He doesn't know I exist. I'm right in his face most of the time being at the ranch, but he seems to be so focused on the stuff going on with the ranch's websites, he doesn't even notice I'm there. I think I'm becoming one of those creepy stalker chicks because I watch him all the time. He's not like the others. I mean, yeah, he's a cowboy and all, but he's not in-your-face macho like Jackson or Joey. He's sweet, kind, and gorgeous."

"Oh, you've got it bad."

Mandy sighed. "You think so? What the hell am I going to do?"

"We'll figure out something. Maybe my dad's right, he needs to be knocked upside the head to realize what a catch you are."

"Maybe."

"A smack would do the man good."

"I like how you think." She tapped her fingers on her lips for a moment. "I could seduce him."

"That's not going to get you a long-term relationship with the guy. They get those kinds of offers all the time. You need to be all he wants in a woman, but play it hard to get too."

"Will you help me?"

"Of course. We're sisters in this!" Callie had finished her own food some time before, so she pushed her plate to the side as they shook hands. "Those Young boys don't stand a chance!"

"But I thought you didn't want to give into your feelings for Jeremiah?"

"I love the man. What can I say? He's had me tied up in knots since I was a freshman in high school and I just can't seem to get away from him even if I wanted to."

"So you want him?"

"Hell yeah, I want him, hogtied to my bed would be a good start, but I have to convince him I can be the woman he wants for the rest of his life. I'm not quite sure how to go about doing that, but I think me not giving in to his sorry ass last night went a long way to convincing him he might want to see where things will lead with us."

"How about we kidnap him?"

"Who? Jeremiah or Jonathan?"

"Both?"

Callie laughed, feeling better every second she talked with Mandy. "Sounds about right to me."

"What are you two conspiring about over here? Those smiles tell me you are up to no good and if it has anything to do with my nephews, I want to hear it."

"Will you warn them?"

She leaned on the table edge with her hands under her chin and a gleam in her eye. "Hell no! I'd love to see every one of those Young boys tied to the woman they were meant to be with. It means doing a little on my part, I'm all there."

"I can't believe we're doing this."

The twinkle in Mandy's eyes told the whole story. She was into corralling herself a Young brother, whatever it took. Callie had to admit, she wanted Jeremiah something fierce, but was she ready to do the necessary thing to convince him he might just want to spend the rest of his life with her? Was she ready for that kind of commitment with him herself? Love did funny things to people's hearts and she was about to find out what it meant to truly love someone.

Chapter Six

Callie sighed as she hung up the phone for the third time in less than an hour. Every guy in Bandera seemed to have her number. She couldn't even begin to understand why all of a sudden she'd become one popular lady, but she had. Just to show Jeremiah she wasn't going to wait for his ass, she'd taken a couple of dates over the last several weeks. Unfortunately, they all turned out to be jerks wanting to get into her pants. *I wish I could remember more about that night at The Dusty Boot.* She must have really been wild. To think Jeremiah took her home so nothing bad would happen to her. She really needed to thank him for protecting her because if the few dates she'd had were any indicator, she dodged a bullet that night.

Her cell phone jingled and she rolled her eyes, hoping it wasn't another guy calling to try get laid.

"Hello?"

"Callie?"

"Jeremiah?"

"Yeah."

"How are you?"

"Okay. I've been working a lot at the ranch, but I wanted to see if you were still mad at me."

"Of course I am, but you're a guy. I shouldn't have been surprised by your actions."

"I really am sorry I didn't at least call you."

"So am I."

The line echoed from the silence for several uncomfortable moments. The background noise was hard to distinguish, but it almost sounded like he was at Anne's diner. She smiled thinking Anne might have put him up to this phone call.

"How've you been? I haven't even seen you at the garage in the last few weeks."

"I've been there, but I've been really busy. I've taken time off."

"Busy how?"

"My phone has been ringing nonstop. I've been out on a few dates. You know. Nothing special." She looked down at her nails for a moment. "Except one." *I am so going to hell for lying.*

"Dates as in plural?"

"Yeah. I had a pocket full of phone numbers the next morning and apparently I gave my number to several guys at the bar."

"I think you did too, but I made sure none of them took you home. You were pretty wasted doing tequila shots."

"I know." She shifted the phone from her left ear to her right. "Um, I should thank you for the lift, I suppose."

"It's okay. It wasn't anything special. I wanted to make sure you made it home okay."

"I appreciate it anyway."

"You're welcome."

Another long pause in the conversation where she wasn't sure what else to say followed until an idea sent off sparks in her brain. "Well, I should go. I have a date tonight. I need to make myself beautiful."

"You do?"

"Yeah. This is our third date over the last couple of weeks." She shrugged even though he couldn't see it. "Who knows? He might get lucky tonight."

A strangled cough echoed through the phone line, making her smile. She was getting to him. *Good.*

"Wait, Callie. You shouldn't be havin' sex with someone you hardly know. It's probably not a good idea."

"Oh, you're one to talk, mister. Besides, who are you to judge?"

"Well, I mean, you hardly know the guy, right? Not like us. We've known each other for a long time."

"And we aren't having sex."

"No, we aren't, but at least you would have known me longer than three weeks."

"It'll be fine, Jeremiah. It's not like I'll be comparing you two." She sighed. "I really should go. He's going to pick me up in like thirty minutes. I haven't even showered yet. I'll talk to you later. Thank you again for helping me. You're a great friend."

After she hung up the phone, she stared at the thing for a minute trying to figure out what the hell she was going to do now. She didn't really have a date for tonight, but now she'd better find one and fast. She looked through the stack of numbers sitting on her nightstand, picking out a name she knew. Brad Smithson, football player from high school. He'd do. He was a big guy, not bad-looking, nice body, and dumb as a bag of hammers.

With a few touches of her fingers, she dialed his number and waited for him to pick up.

"Hello?"

"Hey, Brad. It's Callinda Lewis."

"Well, hey, Callinda. How are you, darlin'?"

She cringed as the endearment rolled over her. Everyone in Texas called everybody else darlin', but she wanted it to only be Jeremiah. Only if he cared. "I'm doin' fine. Listen, I know we haven't talked since the night at The Dusty Boot, but I was looking for someone to do a few body shots with tonight. I wanted to know if you were game?"

"Oh hell yeah, baby. I'll be game to suck on you any time of the day or night. What time shall I pick you up?"

With a shudder, she said, "Why don't we meet at the bar? I need to have my own car there."

"I can take care of you, honey."

"I'm sure you can, Brad, but I have a friend who might be there too and if she gets into trouble, I need to be able to take her home. You remember Mandy from that night, right?"

"Yeah. Pretty blonde with the pink stripe in her hair."

Callie laughed. "That's her."

"Okay. No problem. I'll meet you there at seven?"

"Perfect. See you in a few."

She hung up the phone with a smile on her face. Jeremiah needed a little dose of his own medicine. Brad would do nicely for what she had planned.

When she pulled into the bar about an hour later, she noticed there weren't too many vehicles around. Of course, for a Tuesday night this seemed pretty busy. Tonight she didn't have any plans on getting shit-faced drunk, but she did plan on giving Jeremiah something to think about. Not knowing whether he would be there, she had to hope Jeremiah actually cared enough to come to the bar or at least find out what she was up to. *Please God, let him care enough.*

She climbed out of her car and headed toward the bar hoping she'd meet Brad by the door. If Jeremiah was there, she wanted to be coming in with Brad, not meeting him there.

Off to her right, she grinned as she noticed a big silver dually pickup sitting near the back of the parking lot. Jeremiah. He'd come. Maybe he did care, even just a little.

Good. She was going to give him a show he'd never forget. Hopefully jar him into making a move toward something they might be able to work on together.

Brad came across the street where he'd parked his truck. "Hey, Callie. Right on time."

"Hi, Brad."

He leaned in to kiss her, but she turned her face so he grazed her cheek with his lips. "You look great!"

"Thanks. Nothing special."

"You still look hot. Did I tell you that before because you do. I mean, when you were here a few weeks ago, you were like totally hot. I didn't get my turn to do body shots off you, and man, did I want to. Maybe tonight?"

"Maybe." She took a couple of steps away from him. "Let's go inside. I could use a drink."

She pulled open the door, letting the cool darkness wash over her before the blinding stage lights hit her in the face.

"Sure thing, babe."

They stopped inside the door to let their eyes adjust. The bar sat off to the right with barstools lining the mahogany expanse for the patrons. Several tables took up the left side with the pool tables and dart boards near the back. There was a large dance floor where a few couples two-stepped their way around the divided area.

No sign of Jeremiah.

"Let's find a table."

"Sure, babe."

She blew out a breath on a heavy sigh. This was going to be a long night at this rate.

When they found an empty table, she waited for Brad to pull out her chair, but he took the other one, flipped it around and straddled it. She shook her head as she grabbed the chair for herself.

"What'll ya have?" the waitress asked, giving Brad an eyeful as she bent over allowing her tank top to gap open around her breasts.

"I'll have a beer. Bud Light in the bottle, please."

"I'll take a shot of Jack."

"Comin' right up." The waitress sauntered back toward the bar where Peyton was working one end while Dan worked the other.

Peyton waved at Callie before she glanced at her date, frowned and tipped her head to the right. Callie wondered how much Mandy had told Peyton of their plans to corral a couple of Young boys. She hoped Mandy hadn't told her much. After all, she was married to one of them and might be a little more apt to be on their side, right? Except Peyton might want to see her brothers-in-law with wives of their own. What better than to have two of her friends hook up with them?

Callie glanced to the right. Ah, there he was sitting back in one of the dark corners, brooding with a beer. Well, too bad. She had plans for tonight and they included going home with one hot cowboy, preferably Jeremiah Young.

* * * *

Jeremiah sat with his hat pulled down hoping Callie wouldn't see him as he nursed his beer, bringing it to his lips for a small sip. He needed to see who she was going out with so seriously they had three dates in the last couple of weeks. Not knowing why, he had a morbid curiosity to see the man she had the hots for, or so he thought.

"Fucking Brad Smithson, really?" The guy had barely enough brains to fill a thimble. "The man couldn't even pass basic math."

Jeremiah squinted as he watched the couple take a seat at a table near the middle of the room. He scoffed when Brad didn't pull out Callie's chair for her. *Figures. He's got no manners at all. My mom would box my ears for not pulling out a lady's chair.* After they ordered drinks, Callie tried to start a conversation with Brad while he watched every other female coming through the door. *Dickhead.*

Thoughts of walking over there, jerking her to her feet, tossing her over his shoulder and spiriting her away to his room crossed his mind. But he couldn't do any such thing. Could he?

More people walked into the bar with waves and hearty hellos to the bartenders as they passed. Most found a table as the waitresses worked the room. Some danced. Some played pool and some worked the dart boards like they wanted to stab someone in the eye.

The entire time Jeremiah's gaze rarely left Callie. She'd dressed to kill in a tight s kirt and silky-looking loose tank top with a gauzy looking sweater over the top. She'd put her hair up in a little updo that made him want to take it down to run his fingers through the silky strands. Her blonde hair normally hung to the middle of her back the few times he'd seen it loose. He liked to watch the curls flowing behind her.

Her lips parted softly in a smile as she appeared to be shyly taking in whatever Brad had to say. Brad grabbed the back of her chair, scooting it closer so he could wrap an arm around Callie's shoulders.

Jeremiah wanted to hit someone or break something when she leaned into Brad's embrace. With fists clenched, he punched his thigh to relieve some of the pressure.

Joshua and Joey slid into the booth next to him.

"What's up, Jeremiah?" Joshua said.

"Nothin'."

"You look pissed enough to bite someone's head off."

"I am."

"Why?" Joey asked, taking a sip of the beer he'd set on the table until he followed Jeremiah's gaze. "Ah. Callie hooked up with someone else?"

"I don't care."

"Sure you do, that's why you are about to chew the end of your beer bottle off every time you take a sip," Joshua added. "Easy, cowboy. She's workin' you."

"She's here with that bozo."

"And playin' you like a fiddle, brother."

"How?"

"You can see how she's not really into what she's doing. We can. We've been watching this whole thing unfold from the pool table area while we played."

"What are you talkin' about?"

"We've been here almost every time she's been here. She's never once shown up with Brad, but she's acting like she's all into him. She's not comfortable. When he leans in, she's not meeting him halfway, she's pulling back."

Jeremiah watched a little closer, taking in the whole scene in front of him. Brad paid more attention to the women walking by, checking out their asses rather than paying attention to the woman he was with. Callie touched his arm, although her hand shook a little when she did, like she was totally out of her league. "She knows I'm here."

"Hell, yeah, she knows you're here, sulking in the corner like some loser."

"I'm not a loser."

"Then take control of the woman you want instead of sitting over here."

"She's out with another guy."

"One she doesn't want to be with, clearly," Joey piped in, putting in his two cents worth of advice to his older brother.

"Like you two are experts in the love department."

"Love, hell! You want to get in that girl's pants, don't ya?" Joshua asked, punching him in the shoulder.

"Yeah."

"Then go over there, pick her up, throw her over your shoulder and take her home. It's what she wants, I'm telling you."

"How do you know?"

"Mandy."

"Mandy?"

"Yep. She's had a few beers. She's been talkin' about you two a lot since she's been hanging out with us by the pool tables."

"Are you sure?"

"I'm sure, bro. Take control of the woman you want. Otherwise, you're gonna lose your chance."

"Move." Jeremiah shoved Joey out of the way so he could get up. He was done pussyfootin' around with Callie. He definitely wanted to screw with her, literally. The crowd between him and Callie's table parted as he made his way to her. Without a word, he took her arm, brought her to her feet, shoved his shoulder into her stomach and hefted her over his shoulder.

"What the hell are you doing?"

He didn't answer, just smacked her ass after he trapped her legs against his chest. Take control. Oh, yeah. He planned to have her hogtied to his bed inside of about fifteen minutes.

"Ouch. You asshole!"

She started hitting his back with the palm of her hand, although she wasn't hitting hard enough to do any damage.

"Jeremiah, put me down."

The crowd clapped as he made his way outside to his truck. "Are you gonna behave?"

"Behave? I'm not the one acting like a caveman. Put me down."

"Not until you promise not to take off. Otherwise, I'll hogtie you with my belt and don't think I can't do it. Remember, I'm a cowboy to the core." She huffed a few times while he waited next to the door of his truck. "Callie?"

"Fine. I won't run."

"Promise?"

"I promise."

He set her inside the cab of his truck on the seat once he had the door open.

"Where are we going?"

"My place."

"Why?"

"We need to talk and I don't want an audience."

"I was on a date, Jeremiah. How dare you manhandle me. This behavior isn't becoming of the gentleman I thought you were."

"I'm not gentleman around you anymore. You want it rough, baby, you got it." He slammed the door before he went around to the driver's side of the truck. When he glanced through the windshield, he thought he saw a little smile curving her tempting lips.

She wanted the roughneck. Well, she got him.

She was quiet on the way to his place. He glanced over at her side of the truck on several occasions to see her sitting with her arms crossed over her ample chest as she tapped her foot on the floorboard of the vehicle. *What is she thinking?*

"Are you going to talk to me?"

"What do you want me to say? I wanted you to manhandle me out of the bar, showing off my ass to the entire town? No, I didn't."

"Why were you there with Brad?"

"I told you, we had a date."

"You made it sound like you'd being seeing him for several weeks."

"Yeah."

"I know for a fact you haven't. Was tonight the first night you'd been out with him?" He tapped his fingers on the steering wheel. "And don't lie to me, Callinda. I know the truth."

"Then why ask me?"

"Because I want to hear from your lips why you felt the need to lie to me in the first place."

"You made me feel like shit, Jeremiah. I wasn't worth your time to even call me to tell me you made other plans."

"Are you still holding a grudge about our date?"

She sighed as she shook her head. "Not really." She turned in the seat to face him. "Do you want to be with me?"

"What do you mean be with you?"

"Do you want to hang out with me? Do you want to be more than friends? Do you want to have sex with me?"

He choked on his own saliva. "Why do you ask that?"

"Because those are the things I want from you, but I'm getting mixed signals."

"Things between us have been messed up from the get-go, Callie. We were friends or acquaintances or whatever you want to call it. I don't know what we are now."

"Well if you don't know, then I don't know either." She sighed as she twisted back around in the seat. "Why did you throw me over your shoulder and haul me out of the bar?"

"I didn't like seeing you with Brad."

"You were jealous."

"No." He pushed his hat off his head as he raked his fingers through his hair. "Yes. Hell, I don't know. I'm confused where you are concerned."

"Do you want to kiss me?"

He hesitated for a moment before he replied, "Yes."

"Do you want to date me?"

"I'm not sure dating is the right word."

"What would you say is the right word?"

His knuckles turned white on the steering wheel as he fought for control. The hesitation lasted longer this time until he finally sighed. "I want to fuck you until you scream my name as you come around my cock."

"Well then."

"Have I shocked you?"

"No."

"Really?"

She tilted her head to the side, giving him a condescending look out of the corner of her eye, he wasn't sure he appreciated coming from her. Funny, it made her all the more desirable because she didn't take his crap. She stood up to him and gave as good as she got.

"Jeremiah, you are the smartest guy I know, but you can be really dumb sometimes."

"What's that supposed to mean?"

"You can do things with numbers I can't even fathom on any level. You are so smart, you scare me sometimes, but really? When it comes to women, you can be really stupid."

"It's normal for a guy not to understand women. Ask my eight brothers."

She laughed, a hilarious, gut-rolling laugh that made him smile even though their conversation was kind of serious. "You crack me up."

"Thanks."

"Okay. Let's get something straight. We've known each other for a long time. If you aren't into serious, I get that. Those kinds of relationships come with time. Time I have on my hands so it's fine, but I'm not necessarily looking for a serious relationship either. If it happens, it happens."

They reached the front of his cabin and he turned off his truck. He wasn't sure where he wanted to go with this conversation. He wouldn't mind seeing how they were in bed together. He had the normal libido of a guy in his twenties. He liked sex, liked it a lot, and if he could find a girl he could have great sex with who didn't get all serious and shit, he'd have it made until he was ready for any kind of relationship. "I'm not ready for serious either. I have too many things to do with my life. I want a girl I can have fun with, maybe get in some great sex. You know, see where we go from there."

She pushed open the door on her side of the truck, stepping out into the gravel before she shut it behind her.

After he stepped out and closed his own door, he went around to the front of the truck to stand in front of her. "This is my place."

"Nice."

"Come on. I'll show you in the inside." He motioned to the other side of the duplex type cabin. "Jackson shares the other side with me, but he's not home right now."

"I saw him at The Dusty Boot."

"He goes there a lot to hang out. He likes the atmosphere, I think. You know. Lots of unpaired women."

"Isn't he a real player?"

"He can be. He's kind of quiet, but very rugged like a cowboy should be. Not like me." After he unlocked the door, he pushed it open to reveal the inside of his space. It was more of a one room place. A desk sat in the corner to the left. His king sized bed took up one whole wall to the right with a deep blue comforter spread over the expanse. He had a small kitchenette type thing back against the wall in center where he could heat up things with the microwave or cook a small meal if he wanted to entertain a woman here. His large television took up the wall just inside the door with his PlayStation game system and two leather recliners. Overall, he loved his space even if it was kind of small. One day he would build a huge house for lots of kids and a wife, but not yet. He had his special piece of property picked out on the ranch at the top of the back hill where his house would overlook the valley below. He'd go up there sometimes to sit while he dreamed of his future.

"You're a cowboy."

"Yeah, but I'm not an in your face kind. I ride and rope. You know, the normal cowboy stuff, but I like the behind the scenes kind of thing more."

She glanced around his space with a look of awe. "Wow. This is cool."

"Thanks. It's not much since it's one room, but I like it."

"You've done great with it." She walked to the kitchenette and ran her hand over the small countertop. "You have your own space. That is awesome."

"The house you have with your dad is great. I like it."

"Yeah, but it's Dad's, not mine. I'm an interloper, so to speak."

"You've lived there since you were born. How can you say you're an interloper?"

She shrugged as she checked out the model cars on his shelf. "It's not mine. I want my own house someday. A big house. Lots of kids, you know?"

The image of Callie sitting on a long porch with a couple of rocking chairs struck him hard. She looked peaceful there with a baby on her lap and a couple more running around playing cowboy in the yard. He could see her, clear as day. The image kind of shocked him since he'd hadn't really thought of her beyond their friendship, but she had him thinking more and more about things outside their immediate situation. "You see yourself as a mom?"

She turned the car over, looking at every minute detail of the model before setting it back on the shelf carefully. "Oh, definitely. I want at least four. Of course, it depends on their father. You came from a big family, but I didn't. I want that for my kids."

"Boys or girls?"

"I don't really care." She walked closer and put her hand on his chest. "I'd love to talk to your mom sometime. I bet it was interesting raising nine boys."

"Including a set of triplets."

"Yeah." Her lips parted as she looked up.

His brain went haywire at the thought of his lips on hers. He wanted it more than anything. "I want to kiss you."

Chapter Seven

"I want that too," she whispered, leaning toward him. "Take what you want, Jeremiah."

Unable to hold himself back any longer, he crushed his mouth to hers in a lip-bruising kiss meant to steal her will to resist. Not that he expected her to after the way she talked, but he didn't want to give her the chance either.

He wrapped his arms around her, pulling her in so her breasts brushed his chest. The kiss deepened as she moaned softly and opened her lips to his seeking tongue. The first touch of their battling tongues sent a rush of desire straight to his groin. He couldn't help it. He craved her with everything inside him. He wanted to lay her across his bed and eat her pussy until she screamed for him. The thought of burying his cock in her sweet heat drove his desire higher still. His cock ached. His balls felt like they were on fire.

As their lips parted, she whispered, "Wow."

"Yeah." Drawing his finger along the scooped neckline of her tank top in a sensual caress, he walked her backward until the back of her knees hit the edge of his bed. "I want you, Callie. I want to fuck you every way but up and then do it again."

"Yes."

"Are you on birth control?" he asked, slowly sliding the strap of her top down her arm.

"Yeah. Have been for a long time."

"Good. I have condoms to protect us both."

"Good thinking, cowboy."

He ran his tongue along the underside of her chin, across her jawline to the shell of her ear. "I'm always prepared to have a gorgeous woman in my bed."

"Had a few women here?"

"Not here."

She leaned back so she could look into his eyes. "What do you mean, not here?"

With a nimble toss, his hat landed on the dresser against the wall. "I don't bring women here. You're the first to see the inside of this room."

"Why me?"

"Because you're special."

"I am?"

"Yes. You aren't just a pussy for me to fuck. You're a friend too. That's special to me."

"Aw, you're such a gentleman, Jeremiah."

Her sarcastic tone was lost on him. He figured she should feel lucky to be with him. After all, he'd given her a compliment, right? He grinned and then leaned in to kiss her again. He liked the feel of her lips under his. The soft curve fit his perfectly. When he pushed to take the kiss deeper, she wrapped her arms around his shoulders, crushing her breasts against his chest. *Dear God*. He wanted her, needed her with every pump of his heart, craved her like he needed his next breath.

The clothes needed to go. The feel of her skin under his hands had his whole body humming with desire as his cock strained against the front of his jeans.

He brought her hands back down to her sides. "Let's get you out of these clothes. I want to see you."

With his fingers hooked in the straps of her top, he slowly slid them down her arms, bringing her shirt with it to bare her breasts. *Wow.* The rose-colored nipples stood up, as if begging for the touch of his fingers.

He cupped both breasts in his hands, sliding his thumb across the nipples until she tossed her head back. A soft moan escaped her lips. "These are gorgeous. I can't wait to taste them."

"Let me get my top off," she said, reaching for the edge of the shirt to bring it over the head. "There. That's better. Now you can play all you want." She toed off her shoes and reached for the button on her jeans.

"I'll get to that in a minute. I want to play with these beauties for a bit first." He pushed her back so she lay across his bed. He wanted to take his time to relish the feel of her skin beneath his fingers. *So soft.* He ran his tongue from the edge of her pants, up her abdomen, smiling against her skin as it jumped from the touch, up to the bottom edge of her breast. She wanted the touch of his mouth. He could tell from the squirming movements, begging sighs and arching of her back. Well, he'd give it to her because he wanted it too. He grabbed both of her hands in his to put them above her head. "Leave them there."

With one breast in each hand, he lowered his mouth to the left one, slowly sliding his tongue over the tip. She sucked in a ragged breath, holding it for several seconds before exhaling in a rush.

"So good."

He flattened his tongue, running it around the areola, slowly circling but not quite touching her nipple.

"You're killing me."

"What a way to die."

"Jeremiah, please."

"Please what?"

"Touch it, suck it, do something. I'm gonna die here." He wrapped his lips around the tip, sucking the hardened nub as she arched her back. "Yes!"

Her nipples were like ripe little berries, sweet and ready for his mouth. He nipped at one to see what she'd do.

"Fuck yeah."

So she liked a little pain with her sex. Good to know.

He sucked the nub into his mouth, flicking it with the tip of his tongue as he rolled her other nipple between his finger and thumb. She moved her hands to his hair, pressing his head harder against her chest.

"More."

He released her breasts much to her moan of protest. "Put your hands back above your head or I'll tie you to the bed."

"Okay." Her hands fisted as she returned them to the spot above her. "I want to touch you."

"You'll get your chance. For now, it's my turn to explore." He stood, positioning himself near her knees as he worked the button on her jeans loose. "Lift up." Her jeans came off with a tug at her hips, leaving only her socks on her feet. He toed off his own boots, and then unbuttoned his shirt.

"I wanted to do that."

"Next time."

"Will there be a next time?"

"I hope to God there is, because I'm totally enjoying myself here." A sigh escaped his lips as he glanced down at her neatly trimmed pubic hair. "You are simply gorgeous." He ran his hands from her knees, up the inside of her thighs, parting them as he went to give him access to the sweet spot he wanted so badly, he could almost come from the smell of her arousal. "I'm going to eat you up."

"Please do," she said, parting her thighs more to give him room to work.

"You like it when a guy eats you out?"

"It doesn't happen very often, but yeah. I love it."

"Good. I plan on doing that very thing until you come all over my face."

"Such a sweet talker."

He growled as he shoved his hands under her butt to bring her closer to his mouth while he knelt on the floor next to the bed. "Spread yourself for me."

With two fingers each on her pussy, she opened the outer lips showing him the little nub already slick and waiting for him.

He took in her scent with a swift inhale right before he took the tip of his tongue and swirled the hardened flesh with it. Her soft moans and arched back told him she enjoyed what he was doing as he licked every bit of flesh under his mouth.

It didn't take long for her moans to turn to cries of ecstasy as he ate at her with fervor. He wanted to taste the sweetness of her cum on his tongue. The need drove his own desire higher than he'd ever felt before.

When she held his head to her center and cried out his name, he knew his life wouldn't be the same after this.

* * * *

Her legs shook, her pussy throbbed, and her whole body hummed as she cried out, "Oh God, Jeremiah!" She'd never had a man go down on her like that, eating at her like he was starving. Jeremiah didn't do anything half-assed, apparently. "Holy shit. That was amazing."

He wiped his face on the comforter right before he stood to strip off his jeans. "Glad you liked it."

"I did. I mean, wow." Her breathing slowed and her heart quit hammering against her breast as she relaxed against the softness of the bed, watching Jeremiah strip off his jeans. "Holy hell! Damn, you're built."

"Thank you." His brow wrinkled. "I think."

She sat up to run her hand from the fur on his chest, down his rock hard abdomen to the cock nestled in the springy curls at the juncture of his thighs. When she wrapped her hand around his cock, he moaned low in his throat.

"I love how you touch me."

"Good." She leaned in to take his cock in her mouth, just enough to envelop the head between her lips.

"Don't tease me."

She slid to the floor on her knees. "Oh, I plan to tease you mercilessly, Jeremiah. I want to suck this, lick it, swirl my tongue around it, and get you so hard you think your balls are going to explode."

"Damn woman."

"Yep."

She sucked his cock between her lips again, rolling her tongue around the head, and then ran it down the length of the shaft. His thighs quivered as he fisted her hair in his hands. His hips pistoned, driving his cock in and out of her mouth in a steady rhythm she knew would bring him to completion before she wanted him to. She let his cock fall from her mouth in a wet slide as she licked down to his balls. "Easy, baby."

"You're going to kill me."

"What a slow, pleasurable death it would be."

"I want you."

"You can have me. Where are your condoms?"

"In the drawer." His breathing seesawed in and out, billowing his chest as he fought for control.

She grabbed one out, ripped it open with her teeth and then rolled the slick latex down his engorged cock. "I can't wait to have this deep inside me."

"Me either, baby. Me either." He lifted her to her feet and spun her around before pushing her down face first into the comforter. "This first time is going to be hard and fast. I can't hold back much longer. Your mouth did a number on me."

She braced herself on her forearms as she spread her legs, waiting for the first penetration of his cock. Good grief, she'd wanted this forever. Now she was finally at the beginning of a relationship with the man she's longed for since she was a teenager on the bud of womanhood. "Fuck me hard, Jeremiah." With a snap of his hips, he buried his cock to the hilt deep inside her. A groan escaped at the first feeling of having him inside her. The size of his cock stretched her to the max. Her body adjusted surprisingly fast since she hadn't been with a man in quite a while. "That's it. Do it."

"God, you feel good."

"Faster," she begged at the slow glide of his movements. "Please."

He smacked her on the right butt cheek. "Shush, woman. I'm enjoying myself here." Wrapping his fist in her hair, he pulled back enough to cause a sting on her scalp as he whispered, "What's my name?"

"Jeremiah."

"That's right, baby. I want you to know who's fucking you."

He continued his slow glide for what seemed like forever.

"You can enjoy yourself next time. I need you to fuck me, damn it."

"Only because I can't hold back."

He began hammering into her like tomorrow didn't exist for them, like this was the first and the last time they would be together. Not if she had anything to say about it. Usually once you got a man in bed, he was there to stay, right? God, she hoped he didn't love 'em and leave 'em. "That's it. Hard."

He reached around her hip to pinch her clit with two fingers, sending her into a spasmodic orgasm she felt clear to her toes. Her pussy clenched around his cock as he continued to slam into her, taking her into a second orgasm before the first one had completely died down. Never in her life had she thought she could orgasm so close together, but there it was. Jeremiah had done it for her, taken her where no man had before.

God, do I love this man.

He shivered when he came apart, pushing against her with an uncoordinated rhythm before he slumped over her back, pushing them both to the bed. "Wow."

"Yeah." She sighed. "Can you get off me? I can't breathe very well with you on me."

He pushed himself up on his hands and rolled to his back beside her. "Sorry."

With his arm slung over his eyes and his body splayed out like a god sunning himself on a rock, she wanted to run her tongue all over him, from his luscious mouth to his cock anyway.

"I'll be ready for round two in a minute, or maybe we should watch television for a bit."

His cock bobbed against his stomach like it had a mind of its own.

"Would I mind having sex again? Hell no."

He moved his arm slightly to peer at her with those gorgeous stormy grey eyes. "You are insatiable, woman."

She giggled as she rolled to her side next to him before tracing a finger through the curls on his chest. "I try."

"Let me get rid of this condom so I can put some clothes on."

"If we're going to make love again, why are you putting clothes on?"

He got to his feet and headed for the bathroom. "I thought we might get something to munch on, watch a little television, and see where the evening leads."

She shrugged as she sat up and pushed the hair out of her face. "Sounds good to me." After she managed to get into her clothes, she padded on bare feet to the small couch in front of his television. "What do you want to watch?"

"Oh, I don't know. There are movies there or whatever is on TV is fine."

She watched as he walked back toward her in all his naked glory. No doubt about it, the man was fine.

Sculpted chest with just the right amount of chest hair, six pack abs, lean legs, strong calves, and his cock was impressive even in its flaccid state.

"You keep looking at me like that we'll be back to testin' the bedsprings sooner rather than later."

"I'm game." She looked him up one side and down the other. "I could use another roll in the hay."

He didn't look happy or content even after just having mind-blowing sex. Something was up.

"We should talk."

"Oh great. The 'we should talk' thing." She crossed her arms over her chest while she watched him pull his jeans over his hips.

"I don't want you reading too much into this, that's all."

"I think we fit pretty good together."

"Me too, but I'm not ready to settle into a relationship, Callie. I'm still working on my future."

"What about dating?"

"We can date."

"Why do I hear a but in there?"

He slid a T-shirt over his head, slipping his arms through the sleeves. "I don't think we should be exclusive or anything. You know. If you want to date other guys to see if things are *the real deal* with someone else, then I'll go along with it."

"You didn't like me out with Brad tonight. What about that?"

After buttoning his jeans, he took the seat next to her on the couch. "Brad is an idiot."

"So?"

"You can do better."

"Better than what?"

"Better than him or me or any other guy in Bandera. You should date some guy from San Antonio or something."

"Why are you trying to get rid of me?"

"I'm not. I just don't want you putting your hopes and dreams on us when I'm not ready. I don't know if I'll be ready for a long time."

"I'm not asking for a relationship, Jeremiah. I don't know if I'm ready either." *You are such a liar!* "But thank you for thinking of me. If you're okay with me seeing other people, then I will."

His eyes narrowed like he contemplated what she said and it left a sour taste in his mouth.

Good. I don't want to date anyone else, but if that's what I have to do to get him to see we should be together, then so be it.

"I think it's the best option. I don't want to be tied down."

"Me either." She nodded. "Good plan, Jeremiah." She stood and walked to the edge of the bed to slip on her shoes. "I think you should take me back to the bar."

"Why? I thought we were going to hang out?"

"Well if I'm going to date other people, I might as well get started. Pickings around Bandera can be scarce. I'm thinking I'll start hanging out in a few bars in San Antonio."

He climbed to his feet and walked toward her. When he tangled his hand in her hair, she almost lost her battle to give into making love again. *No, it's not making love, at least not to Jeremiah. To him, I'm a fuck buddy.*

"I thought we could still see each other. You know, sometimes."

"Sure," she whispered, loving the feel of his hand in her hair. Her breathing sped up. Her heart hammered in her chest.

"Are you going to be fucking other guys?"

"Well." She glanced down until he tugged on her scalp to bring her gaze back to his. "We aren't exclusive, so yeah." Not like she really would. She only wanted him, but he didn't need to know she didn't care to be with anyone else. She almost cried when he let her go.

"All right."

That's not what I wanted to hear. "I appreciate the ride."

He sat on the side of the bed to pull on his socks and boots. "No problem." After a moment, he slipped on a T-shirt over his head, hiding his chest from her view.

This wasn't turning out like she'd hoped when he'd thrown her over his shoulder to take her out of the bar, but what the hell. She'd get him to realize they were meant to be together somehow. *Damn stubborn cowboy.*

Several minutes later, he pulled up next to her car in the parking lot of The Dusty Boot. Several cars had already gone, leaving hers solemnly sitting by itself in the back corner. When he shut the engine off on his truck and popped open the door, she figured their night was over. Not that she didn't want it to continue, she really did, but apparently he got what he wanted and was done with her.

She felt like shit.

"Thanks for the evening, Jeremiah. I appreciate—"
Her words were cut off by his mouth on hers as he
cupped her face.

"I'm not done with you. Remember that when
you're seeing someone else."

"But you said you weren't ready for anything but
friends with benefits or whatever."

"I know what I said."

"You're confusing me."

"Me too. You do what you have to do." He stepped
back, leaving her cold.

She watched him climb back into his truck and
drive away without a backward glance. After she
exhaled forcibly, she pulled the car keys out of her bag,
unlocked the door and slid behind the wheel.

Why did men have to be so damned difficult?

Chapter Eight

Jeremiah sat in the corner of the bar watching Callie as she flirted, danced, played pool, and generally had a good time…without him. He took a sip of his beer barely hearing the woman sitting next to him chatter on about shoes or some shit he didn't care about.

This whole situation with Callie seemed to be slowly driving him nuts. He wanted her so why the hell was she there at the bar without him?

Callie threw back her head and laughed at something the guy next to her said before she leaned over to shoot another ball. She stood up abruptly when the guy ran his hand over her hip, and then across her right butt cheek. The shy little look she gave the guy pissed Jeremiah off. He knew she was no inexperienced virgin. The woman knew how to wind a man up to explosive with her perfect little mouth. He could attest to her prowess in the bedroom.

When she leaned in and kissed the guy on the mouth, Jeremiah about lost his mind. The mouth that was supposed to be wrapped around his cock, not some jerk's she picked up at the bar.

He knew just exactly how many men she'd been out with since their little split and how many times he'd asked her to come over for a bit of a romp. She'd always been too busy going out with someone else when he'd asked.

Damn her.

"Are you even listening to me, Jeremiah?"

He cranked his head around to look at the brunette next to him. What was her name again? Didn't really matter. "Yeah, I'm listening."

"Then what did I say?"

"Something about shoes."

"I was telling you about a particularly cute pair of pumps I bought today at the mall. You should pay more attention."

"Okay."

Her voice melded with the music being played as he glanced back at Callie. She'd wrapped her arm around the cowboy she was playing pool with and kissed him full on the mouth. His gut knotted. She wasn't supposed to be kissing anyone but him, right?

He didn't know anymore. She'd done tied him up in knots with this dating other people thing. It had gone on long enough, he figured.

"Excuse me."

"Where are you going?"

"I need to talk to someone. I'll be back."

"Wha—" The girl sputtered next to him as he slid out of the booth and headed toward Callie.

When he got close he heard her laugh again. The sound went right through him, curling his toes in his boots only to center in his balls seconds later. "I need to talk to you."

"Oh hey, Jeremiah. I didn't realize you were here," she said as the guy next to her stood behind her, kissing her exposed neck.

"Can we talk?"

"Um." She giggled when the guy licked her ear. "I'm kind of busy."

"I see that."

"Maybe later?"

"Now." He grabbed her hand, dragging her across the bar to a dark corner.

"What the hell? I thought we had this manhandling thing taken care of. I mean really." She jerked her hand out of his grasp. "The caveman behavior isn't becoming of you. I thought you were more sophisticated than this."

"What are you doing?"

"I'm not doing anything."

"You're letting some guy climb all over you."

She threw up her hands before settling them on her hips as she gave him a glare. "What do you care? Remember, 'let's date other people,' you said. That's what I'm doing, dating other people."

"He's treating you like a whore."

"I'm not a whore, Jeremiah."

"I didn't say you were." He paced a few steps away from her, and then back toward her. "How many guys have you been out with this week?"

"What difference does it make to you? You didn't want to be exclusive, remember? Your words, not mine."

"How many?"

"Six."

"Six different men this week. How many have you slept with? And don't lie to me, I'll know. You aren't a very good liar, Callie."

She pressed her lips together, dropping her gaze to the floor. "None."

"None?"

"None."

"What is going on here then?"

Her head snapped back up. "I'm doing what you wanted, dating other guys. You are dating other women. I know. I saw you with Melissa at the table in the corner."

"That's her name?"

Her mouth fell open before snapping shut. "You don't even know her name?"

"She probably told me, but I forgot."

"You're a jerk, you know that?"

"What?"

"Exactly what is your problem? You drag me over here away from my date, who by the way I do know his name. It's Craig. We were having a good time, and yeah, I might let him have some tonight if it's okay with you, but really I don't give a damn if it is or not because we," she moved her finger between the two of them, "are not a couple!"

"We should be."

"You started this shit. I'm doing what you wanted so back off, Jeremiah. I'm done playing your games. You don't want me. I get it. Well, other guys do, so I'm going with that."

She spun on her booted heel and headed back toward where her date stood leaning against the pool table waiting for her. *If I was her guy, I would have decked whoever dragged her away from me.* "Well, guess what? You aren't her guy."

He glanced back at the table where he'd left the girl he had a date with tonight. What was her name? Oh yeah, Melissa. The table stood empty. *Maybe she went to the bathroom.* He walked over and took his seat as he waited to see if she came back. Nope. He saw her talking to some other guy halfway across the room. Oh well.

His beer had grown warm, but he didn't care, he needed the alcohol. He signaled for the waitress to bring him another. Maybe he'd go home with someone tonight. Ah, who the hell was he kidding? He tried that on a few occasions in the last several weeks without success. The one woman he wanted was dating other guys at his request. The beer went down his throat with a sour aftertaste. Warm beer sucked.

"Here you go, Jeremiah."

"Thanks, uh…"

"Allison."

"Allison. Thank you." He looked her up one side and down the other with an appreciative eye. "How late do you work tonight?"

"Midnight."

"Wanna go home with me?"

"Are you asking me to sleep with you?"

"Yeah."

She pulled back her hand and slapped him hard across the cheek. "I'm not a slut. The least you could do is buy me dinner before fucking me." She dumped the beer in his lap. "I'll find you another waitress."

"Well, shit." He stood up as beer soaked through his jeans. "Damn it to hell!" Several people around him laughed while he fished the keys to his truck out of his pocket and headed for the door. "Screw it. I'm going home."

"Hey, Jeremiah!" Peyton motioned him to the bar. "You okay?"

"Yeah. Just a little wet and not the good kind."

"I see that. I'll have Dan talk to the waitress."

"No biggie. My fault. I approached her all wrong."

"Seems you've had a problem with that a lot lately."

"Yeah, I guess so." He glanced down at the front of his wet jeans. "I'll see you later."

"Be careful."

"I will."

He pushed out the doors and walked to his truck. Tonight would be a long, lonely night because the woman he wanted was laying it on pretty thick with some other guy in the bar right now.

When he slid behind the wheel of his vehicle, he stopped for a moment to watch the front doors. He could go back in there and demand she come home with him, but no, he couldn't do something so caveman-like. Well he could, and he had, but it wouldn't get him anywhere with her now. She'd already made things pretty clear.

What was it about her that made him want her so much? She wasn't beautiful in a model sort of way. Her beauty came from within. She had a heart of gold. He'd seen it on a few occasions when she'd volunteered over Christmas to be Santa's helper at the elementary school. The chance to observe her good deeds only came once in a while, but he knew she volunteered a lot at the nursing home in town too.

It took a lot to keep her dad's shop running as well. She did that. She worked on cars when she didn't have to. She had the brains to do anything she wanted with her life, but she chose to help her dad keep his garage open. That took guts, determination, and a soul of a woman, the kind of woman he'd like to get to know a whole lot better. How though? She wasn't the pushover type. She didn't go for his lines or his smooth words. She wanted something out of life. What did she really want from him?

She said she didn't want a relationship. Neither did he, right?

He wasn't so sure anymore. He wanted to be stable financially before he got serious with a girl and started a family. Did several million in the bank make him stable enough? His family needed to be there too, although they didn't have as much as he did, they were doing pretty well.

He needed to talk to his parents. Maybe by letting them in on what he'd done with their money, it would make the whole thing seem less significant.

Maybe Mom and Dad will have some words of wisdom for me.

He nodded to himself, started his truck, and pulled out onto the road back to the ranch. A discussion seemed to be the right thing to do in a situation like this.

The ride home left him time to think about Callie. Maybe his mom could give him some insight to his situation with her as well. He didn't know what to do anymore.

Several minutes later, the gates of Thunder Ridge Ranch came into view. The large double wrought iron gates were home and had been since he was born. His parents had bought the place when his older brothers were little. He loved living on the ranch, watching the sun come up over the horizon from the front porch while he sipped hot coffee. Dreams of his future always plagued him though. He had plans, big plans, but the illusiveness of who would share those plans eluded him. Callie's face seemed to be taking the place of those illusive dreams more and more.

The numbers came easy as did the money, but was it enough? Would it ever be enough?

He rubbed the fingers of his left hand. The numbness had returned much to his annoyance.

The lights of the main lodge came in to view as he pulled up into his parking spot in front of his cabin. His place only sat a few hundred yards from the big building housing the dining facilities of the ranch, the huge gathering hall with the pool table, dart boards, massive fireplace, and big leather couches. The comforting feelings of home always calmed his restless soul, well, most days. Today, he wasn't so sure.

He turned the truck off, popped open the door then slammed it shut behind him before he headed up the cement walkway to his cabin. He needed to shower and change clothes before he talked to his parents. He glanced up at the inky black, cloudless sky, wondering what Callie was doing right now. *I can't think about her. It'll drive me crazy.*

Off in the distance he heard giggling children. The ghosts of the kids were out wandering the ranch tonight. He'd never thought about why they were trapped at Thunder Ridge before, but there had to be a story there somewhere. He opened the door to his cabin as the giggling faded into the night.

Darkness surrounded him. Not even a small light in his room to illuminate the black space. Just how he liked it. When the sun rose in the morning, it would drag him from his dreams like it did every day. He enjoyed the quiet time on the porch sipping coffee as the ranch came alive around him.

With two fingers on the lamp, he twisted the knob until the light came on. Scenes of the night with Callie came rushing back. She'd been there, teasing him, coaxing him, and loving him for a short time. He hadn't been able to forget that night for more than a few moments since it happened. Her body cradling him as he drove her to heights of ecstasy, haunted him day and night. His cock stirred to life. This he didn't need when he planned to talk to his parents about money, but it was there nonetheless.

After he stripped off his T-shirt, toed off his boots, and pulled down his jeans, he headed for the bathroom off to the back of his room. A nice hot shower would do him good even if he'd taken one this morning. Hot, sticky sweat clung to his body. The sour smell of beer crinkled his nose as he turned on the water in the shower.

Once he had it the right temperature, he dropped his boxers to step under the spray. The hot water cascaded down his chest, abdomen, and groin washing away the sweat of the day, not to mention the beer dumped in his lap earlier. He grabbed the shampoo from the shelf to wash his hair.

Thoughts traveled precariously to Callie on her knees in front of him like she'd been when she sucked his cock. *Damn, I don't need this right now.* But he couldn't shake the image this time so he let it take him. He grabbed the soap from the dish to scrub his body, letting his imagination run wild with the picture of Callie doing wonderful things to his cock using her mouth.

He wrapped his hand around his cock, stroking it up and down with a firm grip.

Her mouth wrapped around the head as she ran a fingernail around his balls. It felt like heaven and hell at the same time. She sucked lightly, drawing his balls up tight. Moaning deep in his throat, the warmth of her mouth scalded him with heat he could hardly stand to feel. When she licked the length of him, his body shuddered with need. As she went all the way down his length, pulling the entire thing into her mouth, he lost control of his desire, squirting cum down her throat in hot spurts.

A groan escaped him as he slumped against the cool tile wall of the shower, trying desperately to slow his heart rate as the water washed cum from his abdomen. Shivers rolled down his back and his legs trembled with weakness. It had been a long time since he'd had to jack off to get relief from his own desire. Another thing to chalk up to his need for Callie Lewis.

He shut the water off before he grabbed a towel from the rack to dry himself. With it wrapped around his hips, he headed over to put some clean clothes on so he could talk to his parents.

Letting out a long sigh, he shrugged on a clean pair of jeans. He really needed to get Callie out of his thoughts if he planned to do anything but fuck her. She'd taken up residence in his dreams now, driving him to distraction time and time again. *Maybe if I fuck her a few more times, this insatiable need to have her pussy will leave me alone?*

"Yeah, brilliant thought, genius. If it was that easy, I'd have done it already," he said out loud while he pulled on a shirt, socks, and boots.

With a shake of his head to loosen the thoughts of the disturbing woman, he headed out to talk with his parents, hoping it would go well and they didn't get too upset with him for keeping the finances of the ranch a secret.

The walk across the ranch yard didn't take long. A few lights from the other cabins reflected off the cement walkway leading to the big house. Guests were settling in for the night, watching television, playing board games or doing family things. He wanted that someday.

He shrugged before he pushed open the side door leading into the massive dining room where they took their meals. The large living room sat to the left with the big, comfy leather couches in the front of the fireplace. He'd spent many a night in this room growing up, doing homework, wrestling with his brothers, or hanging out talking about girls. He smiled. The memories were good ones.

"Mom?" he called as he headed down the long hallway that led to his parents' private quarters. "Dad?"

"Back here," his dad answered from their small living area. "In the den."

When he came around the corner, he saw his dad sitting in one of the recliners and his mom at the desk typing away on the computer. "Don't you do enough work during the day, Mom? You shouldn't be on the computer after you leave the office."

"But I had one more reservation to look at. Then I'm done. I swear."

His dad raised an eyebrow as he shook his head. "She'll be there for another hour at least, doing one thing or another."

"I need you to take a break for a minute, Mom. I need to talk to you two about something."

"Okay." She shut down the computer screen and turned her chair around. "Have a seat, Jeremiah."

He wiped his sweaty palms on the thighs of his jeans as he took a chair, turning it around so he could straddle it.

"What's up, son?" his dad asked.

"I have something to tell you." He glanced up at the ceiling before facing his parents again. "I've been investing for the ranch."

"Investing?" Nina asked.

"Yes. Stocks, bonds, oil. Those kinds of things."

"We trust you to do what is best for the ranch, Jeremiah. That's why you are in charge of the finances."

He blew out the breath he wasn't aware he'd been holding until then.

"Exactly what are you saying?"

"There is enough money in the ranch account for you to close down and retire if you wanted to."

"Just how much are we talking about?" James tapped his foot on the floor, a sure sign of concentration on his part.

"There is five million in the ranch account."

"Five million?" Nina's shocked face almost made him laugh. What would she say when she found out how much he'd amassed in his own account?

"You said five million, Jeremiah?" His father stopped tapping.

"Yes."

"You've invested enough of our money to make five million for the ranch and you think we'd be mad? My God, son, that's fantastic!" James jumped to his feet and dragged Jeremiah to his feet for a hug. He slapped him on the back with a laugh. "You've done well, son."

"I shouldn't tell you how much I have in my own account."

"More than what is in ours?" his mother asked, surprise written in her eyes.

"Yes. My account has double that amount."

"Why the hell are you still working for us then? Not that I want to lose you as our financial person especially knowing you've managed to make us rich, but you could do so much with your own. Your future is secure."

"I know, but I don't know if it's enough."

"Why not?" Nina dabbed at her eyes as a lone tear trickled down her face.

Why was she crying? He hoped she was happy for all of them, but he couldn't be sure. Nina didn't cry much. He could remember a handful of times during his entire life. "What's wrong, Mom?"

Sobs shook her shoulders. "I'm so happy. I worry about this place from month to month. You've taken a huge load off our shoulders, Jeremiah. You have no idea how relieved I am." She wiped at her face. "Now back to why you don't think you have enough money."

"I think I do, but then I want so many things to be perfect before I worry about taking on a wife and kids. You know?"

"Is there someone specific you are thinking about marrying?"

"No, but I think about it a lot. When I find the right girl, I want to be able to provide for her and our children for the rest of their lives." He held up his hand when his mother went to say something else. "Not that I had a bad childhood. You and Dad provided for us more than we ever wanted, but I want my kids to be able to go to college and not have to pay for it. I want to be able to help them start a business if they want to. I want my wife to not have to work if she doesn't want to. That kind of stuff is important to me."

"Son, if you've found someone you want to marry, what you are holding out for won't be so important."

"I don't think so, Mom." He wiped his hands on his jeans again.

"Is there something else?"

"I feel kind of stupid."

"Why?"

"You know I took Callie Lewis out."

"Yes. I trust you had a good time?"

"Well, not so much. She tried acting all weird. Like some of the other girls I'd been out with. It wasn't right. I told her she needed to be herself. We spent the evening watching movies and eating popcorn."

"Sounds like a nice date."

"It was. Then we were supposed to have a date the following evening, but I screwed up. You remember telling me to call her?"

"Yes."

"Well, I forgot. She was pissed I stood her up."

"I don't blame her."

He raked his fingers through his hair before putting his hat back on his head. "I don't either. I went to the bar to apologize, but she shut me down."

"Again, I don't blame her."

"I know. I fucked up. I wanted to make amends. She got pretty wasted that night. Did some things I'm sure she wasn't proud of. Anyway, she said she was dating someone. I checked it out when they met at the bar. I did something stupid again."

"And?"

"I hauled her over my shoulder, brought her back here and we had sex."

His father's eyebrow shot up, but his dad didn't say a word.

"I know. Not good, but it happened. Anyway, we kind of argued about what I wanted in life. How I wasn't ready for a relationship. We agreed to start dating other people, but the plan has backfired on me."

"Oh?"

"Yeah. She's having a blast while I'm miserable. I've tried dating other women, but they aren't measuring up to her."

"Sounds like you have an infatuation with Callie Lewis," his father replied, coming into the conversation for the first time. "Are you sure you aren't halfway in love with her?"

"No way, Dad. I can't be."

"Why not? You've known her for a long time. You've been friends for a long while and now you're lovers or were anyway. How is it hard to come around to being in love with her?"

Jeremiah jumped to his feet, pacing back and forth a couple of times in front of his parents. This was crazy. He couldn't be in love with Callie. In lust, yes, but in love, no. Not possible. *Why not?* It can't happen like this. He liked her a lot and they were pretty good in bed together, but in love? "I like her."

"I'm sure you do."

"We were pretty good in bed together."

"You've had that before, though. You've had a pretty active sex life for quite a while."

He didn't like talking sex with his parents, but yeah, they were right. Good together in bed didn't make for a healthy relationship.

"What is it about Callie that makes her so different to you?"

"I'm not sure. She gets me. She knows me. She's not afraid of the angry me, the me who kids around, or the me who shows off."

"Does she know about your money in the bank?"

"No."

"Then you know she's not after you for your money."

"She's not after me at all, Mom. She seems indifferent to being with me now, much to the detriment of my ego." He raked his fingers through his hair before putting his hat back on his head. "Fuck."

"Is it the fact she doesn't act like she wants you that has you attracted to her? You know, the want what you can't have scenario?"

"I don't think so. I mean, I like her. She's funny, smart, kind, gorgeous, good with kids, helpful to other people even if it means she loses something in the end."

"Well, I think you should continue to stay away from her. Clearly, she's not the girl for you." The smirk on his mother's face told him she was kidding, but the thought of not seeing her made him sick to his stomach. "Oh, and watch your language, mister. We don't talk with such dirty mouths around here."

"Sorry. I'm upset right now and my mouth gets away from me."

"Well, see that you curb it a bit."

"Yes, ma'am."

Chapter Nine

Callie watched Jeremiah leave with a heavy heart as Craig continued to kiss her neck from behind. The disinterest she felt in having the other man even touch her crowded her heart. She didn't want Craig. She didn't want any other man but Jeremiah. He was driving her nuts with his behavior though. First he didn't want her, then he got pissed because she was with someone else, then he did want her. *What the hell?*

"Yo, Callie?"

"Sorry."

"It's been a long time since I've been with a girl who didn't want to be with me."

"It's not that."

He tipped his head in the direction of the door. "Jeremiah?" he asked, moving around so he could look into her eyes.

"Yeah." She dropped her gaze to the tips of his boots. Disappointment raced through her. She didn't use people, but this felt like she'd been using the men she'd been out with since Jeremiah's statement about dating other people. She didn't want anyone but him. How in the heck did she convince him they belong together? "I'm sorry. I've been a really bad person this week. I don't normally do this kind of thing, but…"

"It's okay. We can be friends."

"Thanks, Craig."

"Sure." He trailed his fingers down her cheek. "Do you want another beer?"

"That would be great. Thanks."

She watched him walk toward the bar, stopping every few feet to talk to someone or another. Craig was a pretty popular guy in Bandera, a great catch, so why couldn't she get into someone like him and not the guy who didn't want her?

"You know he wants you as much as you want him, right?" Joey whispered in her ear from behind.

Startled, she swung around, almost hitting his shoulder with her nose. "Sorry. What did you say?"

"Jeremiah. He's being stubborn, but he wants you as much as you want him."

"How do you know?" she asked, leaning on the pool table.

"I've seen the way he watches you. When he took you out of the bar a few weeks ago, he almost had steam coming out of his ears watching you with Brad."

"Then why doesn't he just give in?"

"Because he's a Young. We don't do anything the easy way. And love? That's the worst one of all for us to admit."

"You're one to talk, Joey. You don't have a girlfriend either."

"No, but I'm always looking. I'm a little young to be settling down yet."

"No, you aren't. You aren't that much younger than me."

"Maybe I'll be *your* boyfriend." He waggled his eyebrows. "You know, I'm better than Jeremiah in the sack."

She laughed and shook her head. "Joey, you are so full of shit, your eyes are brown."

"Why, yes they are." He laughed along with her as he drew her into a hug. "He'll come around."

With her arms wrapped around him, she hugged him tight, hoping he was right. "I hope so, Joey. I wish I knew what to do to make him see me as the woman for him."

"He will."

Craig brought her back her beer finally. "Are you makin' a move on my girl, Young?"

"Nope, but she ain't your girl."

"She is tonight."

"She belongs to my brother."

"Well, he hasn't figured out what the hell he's missing yet, so for tonight she's mine."

Joey's eyes narrowed and Callie thought the two men would fight if she didn't do something quickly. She stepped between them, putting a hand on each of their chests. Joey and Craig were close to the same height, but towered over her by at least several inches. She didn't care. She wouldn't have them fighting over something that wasn't their concern. "Easy, boys. This isn't your fight. You're both right, but tonight I'm here with Craig. He's being a perfect gentleman, Joey, so calm down. Nothing worth fightin' over here."

"But—"

"Nothing, Joe." She stepped in front of him and put both hands on his shoulders. "Stop and listen to me. What's between me and Jeremiah is just that, between the two of us. I know you love your brother and want to see him happy. I get that, but fighting other men over me isn't going to change the situation."

"You should be with him."

"I know that. So does Craig, but he also saw Jeremiah walk out of here without a backward glance."

"I saw your conversation with Jeremiah. Neither of you looked happy."

"We weren't. He was trying to tell me who I could see and who I couldn't after he told me to date other people. I'm doing what he asked. I'm sorry if he doesn't like it."

"He's being an idiot."

"I know this and so do you. So does a lot of people in this bar, but he has to come to the same conclusion before he'll change the way things are. For now, we live with what he has decreed."

"You are too good for him."

"Thank you." She put a hand on his cheek. "You'd make a great brother-in-law."

"When he finally figures out what he's missing, maybe, until then I'm on your side of this fight. I'll do what I have to so you two can be together."

"I appreciate your support. Really." She stood on her tiptoes and kissed him on the cheek. "Now what do we have to do to find you a girl?"

"No, no. Not me."

"Oh, yes." She glanced around the bar, but didn't see anyone she thought would fit the tough as nails cowboy in front of her. The man rode horses for a living, bucking and kicking horses. She was amazed he still seemed to be in one piece.

"Forget it, Callie. I don't need one woman. I need a few."

"Well, I don't see anyone here good enough for you. I'll keep my eye out though." When she glanced back to the bar, she saw a dark-haired woman talking with her hands to some guy sitting on a bar stool. *Wow. I wonder what that's all about?*

"I'll leave you to your *date*, but I'll keep an eye out for you too."

"Thanks." She watched Joey walk toward the bar and take a seat next to the woman she'd seen a little bit ago and then turned to talk to Jackson who had one hand wrapped around the waist of some leggy blonde. Leave it to the Young brothers to have women hanging all over them. "I'm sorry about that, Craig. You know how those guys are."

"Yeah, I know. I've had a run-in with one or two of them before." He picked up the pool cue. "Shall we play another game or two while we waste a few hours here at the good old Dusty Boot?"

For the next few hours she drank, laughed, shot pool, threw some darts and generally had a good time. She didn't think of Jeremiah more than a million times during the time period, or so she thought.

She found she really liked Craig as a friend. If she hadn't been in love with Jeremiah, things would have been a lot easier, but alas, she was, and she would have to deal with it.

* * * *

Jeremiah stared at the computer screen in his cabin. He did his own trading with stocks on his own computer so he didn't mix business with personal stuff. Soft country music played in the background while he watched the numbers change and blur. He squeezed his eyes shut, rubbing them with his fingers to try to bring everything back into focus. He really needed to see an eye doctor, he figured. These episodes of blurry vision were getting more frequent. Not that anyone in his family had vision problems, but there was always one.

Two fingers on his right hand tingled like they were going to sleep. He rubbed them with his left to bring the feeling back into them. Things like this had been happening more and more, he noticed recently. He probably needed to see the family doctor. After all, it had been several years since he'd had a physical, probably the last year of high school so he could run track. Cross country running was the only sport he'd done in high school. Running long distance gave him time to think, lots of time to think.

The numbers are the screen came back into focus. He was doing well. His bank account was steadily increasing as well as the family finances. Complaining at all didn't seem right. He smiled as he flipped off the computer to head to bed. It was midnight and he had to be up early for cowboy call as he named it. He had wrangler duties tomorrow and Joey wanted his help breaking a new mare he'd recently purchased. The duties on a ranch never ceased.

After his talk with his parents, he'd headed back out to his cabin for some me time. He didn't get enough of it with a large family. Tonight he wanted to veg out in front of the television and *not* think about Callie Lewis.

He shook his head to dislodge the thoughts of her, but it was difficult since he'd fucked her hard over the side of his bed. Those images wouldn't leave him alone.

A sigh escaped his lips as he climbed to his feet. Dizziness swamped his head for a moment as he grabbed the back of his chair for balance. These symptoms were coming more frequently. A doctor's visit needed to happen soon. This wasn't normal for a twenty-eight-year-old guy. He'd make an appointment tomorrow, well, today when he woke up.

After checking the time again, he decided to hit the bed. His duties required him to be up by seven in the morning for breakfast and rides, then working with Joey on the horse. Maybe he'd throw some hay tomorrow or something to work off some of this frustration he felt. Couldn't hurt, right?

He stripped off his jeans, tossed his T-shirt over the back of the chair and then climbed under the cool sheets. Lucky for them, they had air-conditioning in all the cabins. He'd die in the summer heat without it even though fall was in the air. He liked to sleep with a very cold room. The moment his head hit the pillow, he drifted off to sleep as dreams clouded his thoughts, dreams of Callie.

She walked in through the door of his cabin wearing a silky blouse and short shorts. Her tanned legs went on forever as she strolled toward him with a smile on her lips. "Jeremiah."

"Callie. What are you doing here?"

"I came because I want you."

"Want me?"

"Bad, cowboy."

"Come closer."

She straddled his legs, bringing her pussy into warm contact with his bulging erection. Lord, he wanted her too. More than his next breath. More than food or water. More than anything.

He trailed his fingers down her cheek until he reached her red lips. She nipped at the pads of his fingers with her teeth, sending shivers down his spine. His cock throbbed behind the fly of his jeans. She knew what to do to drive him crazy.

With a tug on the hem of his T-shirt, she pulled it over his head, dropping the soft cotton to the floor beside the chair. Her fingernails raked across his chest until she reached his nipples. The sting of her sharp nails made his skin bust out in goose bumps.

"Do you like a little pain with your pleasure, Jeremiah?"

"Maybe."

She scooted back on his knees enough where she could reach his chest with her mouth. Her teeth sank into the right nipple, sending pain and pleasure shooting straight to his balls. When she sucked it between her lips, he almost came in his jeans. God, she was good.

"I'm going to suck you dry, cowboy."

She shimmied off his lap before she grabbed his belt buckle to undo it. His jeans came next with a tug of her hands at his hips. He raised his ass high enough she could work the stiff material down his thighs to the tops of his boots. She didn't worry about getting them completely off as she dove into giving him pleasure with her mouth. The slick feeling of her tongue as it danced down his cock pulled a deep growl from his throat. He didn't know how she got so good with her wicked tongue, but he loved it. Her fingers worked his balls into a frenzy as she continued to lick, suck and deep throat his cock.

As his balls drew up in the impending climax of his desire, he pulled her off his cock, pushed her shorts to the floor and forced her to straddle his lap. When he sank balls deep into her pussy, his whole world narrowed to the feel of being deep inside her.

Hot wetness surrounded him. The ridges of her vagina caressed him as she slowly rode him.

"Fuck me, baby."

"Oh I plan to, cowboy. I'm gonna ride you into tomorrow."

The slow crawl of her movements had him panting in moments. He couldn't hold back. He needed to come more than his next breath, but he couldn't, not without making sure she had an orgasm along with him. "You need to come along for the ultimate ride."

Her movements sped up. She rocked her hips back and forth, drawing his own orgasm to the tip of his cock before she moaned softly. "I'm right there. Help me."

He reached down between their bodies, rubbing her clit with his finger faster and faster as she continued to rock. His own climax was held in check as he gritted his teeth until he felt her quiver around him. "Come with me, Callie."

"Fuck!" she screamed as her climax broke.

He released the steely hold he had on his own the moment he felt her squeeze him like a vice.

Jeremiah woke up with a start to find cum across his abdomen. *Damn, I haven't had a wet dream since I was a teenager.* He tossed his legs over the side of the bed and struggled to his feet to go to the bathroom to clean up. *Wow. That was intense. It has to be from my forced celibacy the last several weeks.*

Once he cleaned off, he strolled over to his nightstand to check the time on his phone. He wondered if Callie was asleep or out partying at the bar. No, the bar would be closed by now. Was she alone or with Craig?

He crawled back into his bed and lay staring at the ceiling wondering what he should do. Talking to her didn't seem to get him anywhere, but he really needed to try.

That's it. Tomorrow we are going to sit down and have a nice long chat to get all of this out in the open. I'm tired of the way things are so something has to change. Either we are a couple or we aren't. No more beating around the bush, playing Mr. Nice Guy and letting her date whomever she wants. She's mine, damn it! It's about time she realized it.

The jingle of his cell phone startled him. Who the hell would be calling at this time of night? He reached over to grab it, realizing his fingers were numb again. *Damn it!*

The caller ID said Jeff. "What the hell are you doing calling me at this time of night?"

"It's Mom. Joey just called. There's been a bad accident. Get your ass dressed and meet me at the main lodge."

"I'll be right there."

He jumped out of the bed, hopping around on one foot as he tried to put his legs into his jeans. This didn't sound good. Accidents on the back roads of Bandera were bad. After he threw a shirt on, he slipped on his socks and boots before he made a beeline for the door to the lodge. His heart clenched. His mom had to be okay. She just had to be.

The minute he went through the doors, he came to a sliding stop next to the crowd of his brothers to get the scoop. "What's happened?"

"Hang on. We are waiting for Joel and Mesa."

A moment later, the last brother came through the doors. "Tell us."

"Joey called a few minutes ago. Mom was hit head-on by a drunk driver. Right now, she's on her way to the hospital in San Antonio by ambulance. She's not conscious. They don't know the extent of her injuries."

"What hospital?" Jeff rattled off the name of one of the biggest hospitals in the area. "I'm going," Jeremiah said, spinning on his heels to rush to his truck.

"Slow down, Jeremiah. I'm sure we all want to be there, but having the entire Young clan bombard their emergency room isn't what is best for Mom."

"I said I'm going."

"All right, but I think it's best if only a few of us go." The boys all spoke up at once until Jeff raised his hand. "I know you all want to be there, but I think only three of us should go. Dad is already on his way behind the ambulance and Joey, so that would make four. I'll stay here with Terri to make sure the ranch doesn't fall apart. Jeremiah, you go." He pointed to two other brothers. "Jackson, you and Jason go too. The rest of us will stay here. Make sure you call frequently with updates."

"Will do," Jeremiah said, turning to the other two who would be going with him. "We should probably ride together so we don't have all of our vehicles at the hospital."

"Sounds good to me," Jackson replied.

A moment or two later, the three men climbed into Jeremiah's truck to head to San Antonio. It would be a long ass drive without knowing what the hell was going on with their mother. How badly was she hurt? Jeff said she was unconscious. That wasn't a good sign. He'd keep that thought to himself though. Talk amongst the three of them was sobering. They didn't say much, watching the streetlights and empty buildings go by until they hit the interstate to take them into the big city. Luckily the hospital wasn't that far and they made it there in record time as they pulled up into the emergency room parking lot.

Jeremiah quickly called Jeff to let them know they'd made it safely. "Let's hope Joey or Dad are out in the waiting room. I doubt they'll let us back there."

"Right," Jackson answered as they walked in through the double sliding doors.

Joey stood off to the side with his back to the door, waiting.

"Joey?" Jeremiah touched him on the shoulder.

"Oh. Hey."

"How's Mom?"

"I don't know. They haven't told me anything. All I know is she regained consciousness for a few minutes when they put her in the ambulance, but Dad came out and told me she'd slipped back under by the time they got her here."

"Is Dad back there with her?"

"Yeah." Joey pulled his hat off and raked his fingers through his hair.

He wasn't the type to get upset normally, but this had hit them all in the gut. Their mother was the rock of the family. Having her hurt meant someone should die. "Where is the guy who hit her?"

"He's in jail."

"I would hope so."

"I should have stopped him, guys. He was drunk at The Dusty Boot. Drinking hard. I should have taken his keys or something." Joey paced back and forth in front of the door.

"Was it someone we know?"

"I don't think so. I didn't know him before tonight."

"Tonight?"

Joey shoved his hands into the front pockets of his jeans as he exhaled forcibly. "His sister was at the bar trying to get him to go home. He'd had a few beers. Not too many, but we don't know how much he was drinking before she got there." He rocked back on his heels. "I danced with her. In the meantime, he took off. She and I went to find him if we could. We saw the fire trucks take off from the station and followed them. Came up on the scene to realize it was a Thunder Ridge truck. I didn't know Mom was behind the wheel. When they cut her out, she was breathing but not conscious. She regained consciousness while we were there. Asked a few questions and said her leg hurt. When they put her in the ambulance she was awake, but apparently on the way to the hospital, she lost consciousness again according to Dad. They are doing some tests now to see what's wrong."

Jeremiah clapped Joey on the shoulder. "This isn't your fault, Joe. You couldn't have known he would hit someone. You did what you could do to get him off the road."

"It wasn't enough, Jeremiah. What if Mom dies?"

"She's not going to die!" Jackson spoke up for the first time. "Do you hear me? She's not going to die!"

"Easy, Jackson," Jeremiah said as he placed his hands on Jackson's shoulders. "She'll be okay. She has to be."

Their father came through the double doors, walking toward them.

"Any news?" Joey asked.

"She's regained consciousness, but doesn't remember anything. They're taking her back for a CAT scan now to see what's up. She has a concussion at least, but they don't know the extent of it right now. They're concerned with bleeding on the brain. Her leg is broken at the femur so she'll be laid up for a while. They'll probably be keeping her here for a few days. She may need surgery on her leg. They're more concerned with her head at the moment." A tear rolled down their dad's cheek. "I can't lose her, boys."

"She isn't going anywhere, Dad. Trust in God. He has her in His hands now." Jeremiah hugged his dad and then stepped back to see tears rolling down his cheeks. It was difficult to see his dad so broken. They would all be in a world of hurt should anything happen to their mom.

"I know, but it's hard to see her like this. She's so confused."

"Does she know who you are?"

"Yes."

"Then she isn't that confused."

James smiled. "After being together for forty years, I would hope she knew who I was."

The sad look in his dad's eyes hurt Jeremiah's heart. He knew how much in love his parents were. Someday, he wanted the same kind of love, a lifetime wouldn't be long enough.

Chapter Ten

The doctor came out of the double doors. "Mr. Young?"

"Yes?" his father answered.

"We need to discuss your wife's care."

"What's wrong?"

"She has some bleeding on the brain from the accident. Her brain is swelling inside her head."

"What does that mean?"

"She'll need to be admitted into intensive care so we can watch her closely. We're hoping the swelling will reduce on its own, but for now there isn't much we can do. If the swelling gets too bad, we'll have to do surgery."

"Holy shit." Jeremiah's breaths came out short and choppy through his nose and out through his mouth as he tried to control it. Panicking wouldn't help the situation. "Surgery?"

The doctor shoved his hands into the pocket of his lab coat. "Only if it gets bad. If the bleeding stops and the swelling goes down on its own, she'll be fine. Right now, we're monitoring her closely. We'll keep her sedated to let her brain heal. We've put a breathing tube down her throat to make sure she has enough oxygen and to keep her sedated."

The boys gasped.

"It's only precautionary at this point. She could breathe on her own, but we want to make sure the swelling goes down. This will protect her airway while we do that. So far, everything looks good. The bleeding is in some small vessels so they will likely resolve on their own."

"What about her leg?"

"She'll need surgery on it for a repair. We've stabilized it, but we don't want to do surgery until the issue with the bleeding is controlled. A couple of days with the break won't hurt anything. We've contacted our orthopedic surgeon to take a look at her x-rays. He's in complete agreement."

Jeremiah felt like his world had crumbled around him. His mother was hurt. His father was a mess. What else could go wrong?

"If you don't have any further questions, I'll leave you alone. We'll be transferring her to intensive care in a few moments. Then let you know what room shortly." The doctor put his hand on James' shoulder. "She'll be okay, Mr. Young. Have faith."

"Thank you, Doctor."

When the doctor left them alone, the three boys each took turns hugging their father. "She'll be okay, Dad. The doctor said so."

"God, I hope so. I can't lose her, Jeremiah. She's my life."

"I know." His cell phone jingled in his pocket. When he pulled it out, he saw it was Jeff. "Hey."

"What's up with Mom? You didn't call."

"We just talked to the doctor, Jeff. Geez, give me a minute." He told his brothers and his father he would fill Jeff in as he walked away so he could hear. After he gave his brother the report of what the doctor said, he closed the phone and moved back to be with his father. When the nurse came out to tell them what room they had moved his mother to, his father excused himself to go to the intensive care unit as they wouldn't let them all in at once. He told them he would come back out as soon as he talked to the nurse to check on Nina.

The boys took seats in the waiting room as they waited for news.

"She'll be fine. She has to be." Joey leaned forward with his elbows on his knees. "I want to kill the guy who did this. It's a good thing he's in jail."

"Me too," Jackson replied. "I don't see how you didn't kill him right there at the accident scene."

"Trust me. If the cops hadn't already had him in handcuffs, I would have. He was belligerent and self-righteous even though he was being arrested for drunk driving. I feel bad for his sister."

"Was it the same girl who got dumped on the floor?" Jackson asked.

"Yeah. The one I was talking to at The Dusty Boot."

"When you two left, I left too. I took a cab home since I'd had a bit to drink. I must have been right in front of the accident on the road."

"Probably. We hit a couple of other bars looking for him before the fire truck peeled out of the fire house headed for the accident."

"I was in my room when Jeff called," Jeremiah added. "I'd just gone to bed not too long before that."

"I wonder if we should go on home. There isn't much we can do here." Jason adjusted his hat on his head after he'd raked his fingers through his hair.

"I want to see Mom first," Jeremiah answered, with a resounding yeah from the rest of the group. "I hope Dad comes back out soon."

With each brother lost in their own thoughts, Jeremiah couldn't help but compare the four of them. They all had their hang-ups and trials as life went on around them.

Jason had Peyton now. They seemed happy. They hadn't been together long. He hoped his brother enjoyed married life. He'd been kind of against it for a while.

Jackson didn't have a girl and didn't seem to be worried about finding anyone. He did his part on the ranch, but he seemed really interested in the history of the land more so than the rest of them. Jeremiah knew he'd been doing a lot of digging into the past lately.

Joey did his own thing with the horses. He was kind of tied up with the neighbor girl, although at eighteen she seemed kind of young for him. He'd been hot for her for a few years. Jeremiah hoped he didn't get into trouble with hanging around her. Her daddy seemed kind of crazy.

And then there were his issues with Callie lately. He needed to talk to her, but his mom came first. It would have to wait until Nina was better. He just hoped he'd have the time to straighten things out before all hell broke loose or she found someone else. He couldn't handle that if she did.

"Hey, Jeremiah. I saw Callie with Craig tonight at the bar." Joey sat back in the chair with his legs crossed at the ankle.

"And?"

"She didn't seem happy."

"No?"

"When are you going to go after that girl?"

"What the hell is it to you?"

"Because if you don't pull your head out of your ass, you're gonna lose her."

"I plan on talking to her."

"Talking isn't going to get shit done with her. She needs a man to take control."

He narrowed his gaze on his brother, thinking about the conversation at hand. "How would you know?"

"I talked to her. She wants you, not Craig."

"I talked to her tonight too. She basically told me to eat shit and die."

"She was just mad. She's upset because you've been giving her the cold shoulder treatment, or so she thinks."

"No I haven't! I've been trying to tell her she belongs to me."

"Somehow I don't think Callie is the type of woman to be told what to do," Jason added his two cents. "She seems pretty strong-willed. She reminds me a lot of Peyton."

"Yeah, she does," Jeremiah replied. "She doesn't like me giving her orders."

"Have you had sex with her already?"

"Yeah."

"And?"

"It was mind-blowing. We're good together, but I have to make her see we need each other, we complement each other in our personalities. She's a great woman." Jeremiah sat forward. "Did you know she volunteers a lot at the nursing home?"

"Really?"

"So what is the problem here?" Joey asked. "As I see it, you tell her you want her, she drops everything to be with you. Done deal."

Jeremiah laughed so hard, he hurt as he doubled over. "Yeah, somehow that isn't going to work with Callie."

"It didn't work with Peyton either. She's very headstrong."

"Did you know she's become good friends with Mandy?" Jeremiah asked. "In turn I would think that makes her pretty good friends with Peyton. Could be bad news if they got into too much trouble together."

"I'll talk to Peyton."

"Yeah, you do that, bro." Joey laughed. "If I know Peyton at all, she'll tell you to stick it up your ass."

The boys shared a laugh at Jason's expense as he glanced at his phone. "I'm going to call my wife."

Jeremiah thought about it for a moment before he asked, "Did Callie leave with Craig?"

"No."

"She didn't, huh?" He smiled. Maybe things were looking up for him after all. Jeremiah rubbed the fingers on his right hand, hoping to bring some feeling back into them. He was getting kind of worried that they kept going numb on him at odd times. Maybe had a pinched nerve or something. "I should call her."

"No, you should talk to her, but not by phone. This needs to be a face-to-face conversation," Jackson said. "She's important to you, yes?"

"Yeah."

"Then you need to make it a personal talk."

"You're right."

Their father came out several minutes later. "The nurse said you can each go in one at a time. Don't stay more than a few minutes."

"I'm assuming you are staying here, Dad?" Joey asked, getting to his feet.

"Of course. I won't leave her side if I don't have to."

"We'll hold down the ranch." Jackson stood as well. "We should make this fast so Dad can go back in there."

"I knew I could count on you boys."

They each filed in one after the other until only Jeremiah was left. He wanted to see her, but then again, he didn't. He wasn't one for hospitals, and to see his mother with a tube down her throat on a breathing machine messed with his brain. She'd been too lively and giving just a few short hours ago. What was she doing on the road at that late hour anyway? He'd have to ask his father when he had a chance.

The moment he walked in, his heart sank. Tubes and wires strung to the box above her head monitored several things at once. He didn't know what they meant. It frightened him a little. As long as they weren't making loud beeping noises, he figured everything was okay. "Mom?"

The nurse came in behind him. "Talk to her. She might be able to hear you even though she's sedated." She checked a few things, and then turned to leave. "You can stay five minutes."

"Thank you."

"You're welcome."

He picked up his mother's limp hand. "I'm sorry you are here, Mom. When we talked earlier, I never thought you'd be in this shape a few short hours later. You'll be okay though. The doctor said you should be okay." A tear rolled down his cheek, but he wiped it away angrily. "We'll get the guy who did this to you. I promise. He'll pay for hurting you."

Her fingers moved slightly.

"Mom?"

No more movement followed and he realized it was probably an involuntary reflex. It made him feel better though, hoping she could hear him so she would know they were all there for her no matter what it took to make her better.

He squeezed her hand before he walked slowly back toward the door. After several peeks over his shoulder, he finally wandered out to the waiting room where his brothers stood talking softly. "Are we ready to go?"

"Yeah," Joey said. "You have your truck, Dad, so you should be good."

"I'll be sleeping in the waiting room since they won't let me stay in her room. If one of you could bring me some clean clothes at some point, I would appreciate it." He glanced down at the mud on his boots. "I've been wearing these since this morning."

"Will do, Dad," Jackson answered. "We'll see you in a few hours. Some of the other boys might come in rather than us. I'm sure they'll want to see Mom too."

"That's fine. Just tell them what to expect so they aren't shocked when they see your mother. I can't imagine walking in on that without knowing. I don't know if you told them about the tubes?"

"Yeah, I did, so they should be prepared."

"Good. Make sure to tell them they can't stay long."

"We will." Jeremiah hugged his dad before he stepped back. "Tell her we love her and we'll see her later."

"Thanks boys, for being here. You don't know how much this means to me and your mother."

"We're family. It's what families do," Jeremiah answered.

"I know, but you never know how people are going to react when things like this happen. We love you boys."

"We love you too, Dad." The other three murmured in agreement to Jeremiah's statement. He knew his dad was having a hard time in this situation, but their love was strong. They would make it through. "Let's go before it gets too much later. I have early duty."

When they walked into the main lodge three hours after they'd left, none of the brothers had gone to bed. They wanted a full report which between him, Joey, Jason, and Jackson, they got every bit of information the four of them had received.

"I'm going to bed, guys. I have to be up in like three hours," Jeremiah said, stifling a yawn with his hand.

"I think we should all go on to bed," Jeff replied. "There isn't anything else we can do tonight. Dad will call me if Mom's condition changes. We have a ranch to run."

All of the boys agreed, finally filing off to their respective bedrooms and abodes leaving Jeremiah to check the room one last time before he went to bed.

When he finally got to crawl under the sheets, he drifted off into dreamless sleep.

Morning came early for Jeremiah as he rolled over with a groan and smacked his alarm to silence the screech. If the guests wanted a cheerful, smiling cowboy this morning they wouldn't get one, he was afraid. He rolled over to his side and wearily sat up. When he climbed to his feet, his left leg felt numb and tingling, like he'd sat on it and put it to sleep. *This is nuts.* He stumbled a few steps before he regained his coordination and could head for the bathroom. He needed a shower this morning more than he needed anything. He had to wake up somehow and coffee alone wouldn't do it. It was going to be a long day.

After his shower, he walked across the room with a towel slung low over his hips to retrieve some clean jeans and shirt.

A timid knock sounded at his door.

"Just a minute." He glanced out the window to find the woman he stood Callie up for, waiting on his stoop. After he threw on his jeans, he didn't bother with a shirt as she knocked again. "Well hello, Brenda, isn't it?"

She stepped inside his cabin and shut the door.

"Can I help you with something?"

"Yes. I'm a horny guest. You need to take care of your guest."

"Listen, Brenda, I don't think that is such a good idea."

"Why not? You were going to the other night until you got that phone call and then dumped me back at the ranch like yesterday's garbage. I didn't appreciate your treatment of me, Jeremiah."

"I'm sorry, but my mother has a strict policy against us messing with those staying at the ranch. I was following her rules."

"I call bullshit. You had every intention of fucking me out there on our ride."

"Can I be truthful with you?"

She walked him backward until his back hit the wall with a thud. Her hands found his chest with both palms resting flat on his skin. "I wish you would."

"I have a girlfriend."

"Is that who called you?"

"Yeah."

"You were going to cheat on your girlfriend?" She slapped him hard across the cheek. "You lowlife scumbag! I can't believe you were going to cheat on her without any regard to her feelings at all."

"But you—"

"Never mind what I was going to do. I didn't realize you had a girlfriend." She spun on her heels and disappeared through the door with a hearty slam.

"Well, shit."

He rubbed his cheek where she'd slapped him before grabbing a shirt, slipping it on and then going to find his socks and boots. If that didn't wake him up, nothing would.

When he went through the main lodge door several minutes later, he found most of the people who were staying on the ranch already eating. His brothers had already got their food so he went through the line to get his own plate and sit down next to Jackson. "Any word from Dad this morning?"

"No, nothing or Jeff hasn't mentioned anything so I would think he hasn't heard anything." Jackson glanced over at him. "You look like shit, bro, and why do you have a nice hand print on your cheek?"

"Brenda paid me a visit this morning."

"Brenda?"

"The guest I took out riding the other day. I think she planned on a morning romp. I told her I had a girlfriend and she slapped me."

"You don't have a girlfriend."

"Not yet, but I hope to by the end of today. I want to have a nice talk with Callie after all my chores are done."

"I hope you two get things straightened out."

"Oh, I plan to. Otherwise, I might have to kidnap her until she listens to me." He shoveled eggs into his mouth, then sipped the hot coffee he'd retrieved before he'd sat down. "Heaven."

"I think we are all feeling the effects of our late night."

"Yeah, but we had to be there for Dad and each other."

"Tragedy always brings people together."

"We are family. It's what we do."

"You got it, bro."

Jeremiah quietly finished his breakfast as he listened to the conversation going around the family dining room table. The guests seemed subdued today even though he didn't think any of them knew what had happened the night before.

The moment he was finished, he stood, took his plate to the wash bin and headed out to the stable to take his first round of guests on the ride over the hills of their home. The boys all traded off doing rides to give each other a break or to do other things around the ranch, but today he could use the time to think. He had plans to make to woo Callie and let her know she was the girl for him.

The sun had begun to set in the sky when Jeremiah emerged from the barn. He'd done his cowboy duty for the day, but now he needed to check on things with the ranch finances.

Joey walked out of the barn behind him, clapping him on the shoulder as they walked toward the main lodge. "Thanks for the help with the mare."

"No problem. I don't get to do enough of this stuff working in an office most of the time."

"I know." Joey laughed. "You need to spend more time in the sun." He compared the tan lines on their arms. "You're lookin' might pale there, bro."

Jeremiah shook his head as he smiled. It felt good to smile for a change with everything going on in his life. He needed that. The break had done him good. "I know what you mean."

Jeff joined them at the door of the lodge. "I heard from Dad. The bleeding has stopped and the pressure is reducing in Mom's brain. They still have her on the breathing machine as a precaution, but they plan to remove it tomorrow."

"Did some of the other brothers go into town today to see her?"

"Yeah. They been going in shifts so they don't overwhelm the poor nurses with our sheer numbers."

"Probably a good idea."

Mandy came out to ring the dinner bell. "Hey guys. How's your mom?"

Jeff gave her a report as soon as she got the guests heading to the dining room for dinner.

"Good. Sounds like things are looking up."

"Yes, they are. We're fortunate she wasn't hurt worse. She is going to need some physical therapy for her leg, but otherwise the doctors think everything else is resolving well."

"That's awesome. She's a nice lady," Mandy replied, stepping behind the serving trays.

The boys headed toward the family table to wait their turn while the guests filled their plates high with food. Jeremiah smiled. Callie would fit in well with the family. *Whoa! I'm thinking long-term here?* He glanced outside and realized yeah, he was thinking long-term relationship with Callie and it felt good. He hoped he could get her on board with the plan.

Chapter Eleven

Callie sat on the couch in the front room flipping through channels on the television without even seeing what might be on. Her mind dwelled on Jeremiah. She'd heard about his mother's accident the other night and wondered how she was doing. She wanted to be there for him, but she didn't know how to go about doing that.

Talk gets around in a small town. It hadn't taken long for everyone to know about it. She felt bad. Nina was a great lady.

The doorbell rang. "I'll get it, Dad."

She climbed to her feet and walked toward the front door. Her life had been pretty busy since her and Mandy's body shots escapades at the bar. She'd been on several dates, following Jeremiah's demand to date other people, but none of those guys were him. None came close to creating the electric impulses he caused in her every time he touched her. Didn't he know they were meant to be together? *Apparently he's too damned stubborn to realize it.*

The bell rang again. "I'm coming."

She pulled open the door and her jaw dropped open. Jeremiah stood on the stoop with a dozen red roses in his hands, dressed to the nines in pressed jeans, brushed clean boots, shiny belt buckle, white dress shirt, suit jacket and his dress black Stetson on his head.

"Hi."

"Hi."

"I'm here to officially ask you on a date. Get dressed."

She jammed her hands on her hips as she frowned. "What the hell, Jeremiah? You can't just show up at my door, ordering me to get dressed up for you. This is bullshit! I'm not at your beck and—"

He leaned in to kiss her full on the mouth before his tongue swept along the seam of her lips and she melted against his chest. When they parted she was breathless and tingly all over.

"I'm here to wine and dine you. Please? Put something pretty on. I want to spend the evening with you."

A breathless sigh escaped her. "Okay."

He grinned when she stepped back to do exactly what he told her. *I'm a terribly weak woman where he is concerned.*

She headed down the hall to her room to shower and change. He'd just have to wait while she got ready since he'd shown up without calling first. She frowned now that she had her wits about her. How does he get off showing up without calling? What if she had a date with someone else?

Her anger exploded through her as she got into the shower, washed her hair and her body and then grabbed a towel to dry off. Yes, she wanted him. She'd do about anything to have him, but this ordering her around shit was for the birds. *I'll show him!* She pulled out the slinky red dress she'd worn before, high heeled shoes and silky stockings. *He's going to know exactly what he's missing when I'm done with him tonight.*

After putting on makeup and blow drying her hair to a pretty upswept hairdo, she slid into her shoes and pronounced herself ready to the reflection in mirror. "Eat your heart out, Jeremiah."

When she walked back down the corridor to find him standing in front of the picture window looking out over the front yard, she stopped to wonder if she was doing the right thing. He was here to take her out. Maybe he'd already realized he wanted to be with her and this was his way of showing her?

"Jeremiah?"

The look on his face made it totally worth the trouble she'd taken to make herself beautiful. His eyes widened as his jaw hung open in appreciation. "You look fabulous."

"Thank you." She glanced down at her dress, tugging on the hem just a little since it only reached mid-thigh when she stood. "I didn't know where we were going, but since you are dressed pretty fancy, I figured I'd better too."

"I'm taking you somewhere special. We need to have a serious conversation about us, but this is going to be a beginning."

Confusion clouded her thoughts. "Beginning?"

"Yes, but I won't say more until we have some alone time." He ran his fingers over her bare shoulder. "You'll need a wrap of some kind. It's chilly out there."

"Let me grab something out of the closet." When she turned around, she noticed he'd found a vase somewhere in one of the cupboards to put the flowers in. "Thank you for the flowers. They're beautiful."

"They don't compare to you."

"You're being such a sweet-talker tonight. What's up?"

"This is me. I hope you don't mind."

"Not at all," she said, grabbing a wrap from the closet and draping it over her shoulders. "Will this be heavy enough? It's wool."

"Should be. The restaurant is indoors so it shouldn't be too bad." His gazed wandered down her frame from head to toe. "Did I tell you how beautiful you are?"

"Yes, but you can say it again. I don't mind."

"How about if I change it up a bit? You are gorgeous." He leaned in to brush her lips lightly with his own. "I can't wait to get you alone."

Wetness coated her panties at the look in his eyes. Desire. Need. Even something she wasn't sure she wanted to name, reflected in his steely grey gaze. *Just maybe?*

He held out his hand for her to take and she slipped hers into his grasp. Her other hand held a small clutch purse with her cell phone, keys and wallet. One always had to be prepared for a night to go completely wrong when on a date. Not that it would with Jeremiah, but one never knew when they might need to get a cab home.

"Shall we?"

She swallowed, trying to wet her parched throat. She wasn't sure what to expect tonight and the thought scared the crap out of her. "Daddy? I'm going out with Jeremiah. Don't wait up."

"Have fun," her father called from his bedroom.

As they walked out to his truck, she got the feeling tonight was going to be a game changer in their relationship. Something had changed his mind about her, although she didn't know what, she wanted to shout to the heavens in thanks.

Jeremiah opened her door for her before she stepped up to slide inside the cab. He shut the door and then walked around the front of the vehicle to get into the other side. Her appreciative sigh echoed in the silence surrounding her. *Boy, was he sharp all dressed up and looking good.*

After he slid inside and started the truck, she snuck a glance in his direction. The jacket molded to his chest, the white shirt was open at the throat, and the jeans were pressed to sharpness. The ultimate cowboy. "You look really nice tonight."

"Thanks. I wanted to dress up for you."

"Are we going to talk now?"

"No. Let's wait until we are sitting at a nice table with a glass of wine or whatever. I want your undivided attention."

"You have it now."

He laughed. "Good, but I want to be able to look into your pretty blue eyes when we talk."

"Sounds serious."

"It is."

"Won't you at least—"

"Nope. You'll have to wait until we get the restaurant."

She crossed her arms over her chest in a silent pout. She didn't want to wait. It would kill her! Okay, maybe not, but the little grin on Jeremiah's face made her wonder what the heck he might be up to.

When they arrived at the restaurant forty-five minutes later, she realized it was one of the swanky places on the riverfront in San Antonio. She'd never been to this particular restaurant before either, but she knew it was expensive and you had to have reservations to get in.

As they approached the podium, Jeremiah's warm hand rested at her back. "Young. We had reservations for seven."

"Ah, yes, sir. Just one moment. Let me check to see if your table is ready."

As they stood waiting, she leaned into Jeremiah's body a little to absorb his warmth and he surrounded her with his arms. It was a nice feeling.

A few minutes later, the guy returned. "Right this way."

He escorted them to a dimly light corner of the restaurant completely situated off by itself. The table had rose petals sprinkled on it with more on the chairs and even some on the floor. It was gorgeous.

"You did this?"

"Yes."

Tears burned her eyes as she tried desperately not to cry. "It's beautiful." He held her chair as she slid into her spot at the table before she spread a napkin on her lap.

The waiter arrived a moment later with a bottle of wine, showed it to Jeremiah, then poured two glasses when Jeremiah gave him a nod of approval. The whole scene was surreal to her. Why was he doing this she didn't know, but she liked it.

She took a sip of the wine and rolled it around on her tongue before she swallowed. "Very tasty, although I'm not a wine connoisseur."

"Neither am I, but it sounded good when I set this up."

She smiled and looked down at her hands folded on the tabletop. "Nice."

He reached over to take her hand in his. "Shall we talk now or wait until after we eat?"

"Now would be good, but we might want to wait until after dinner. Depending on how this goes, I might not have an appetite."

"I think you'll like how this goes, Callie."

"Okay."

He inhaled like he was trying to steady his nerves before taking a leap into a very deep pool of water. "I think I'm in love with you."

"You think?" she asked, tipping her head to the side.

"Well since I've never been in love before, I'm not certain, but after talking to my parents and brothers, I'm pretty sure, yeah, I'm in love with you." He intertwined their fingers, then rubbed the pad of his finger over the knuckle on her thumb. "I've been miserable without you. After we made love that one time, I haven't been able to get you out of my mind. It's been driving me nuts." He dropped his gaze to the table. "Believe me, I tried. I didn't want to fall in love right now, but alas, here I am. I want you in my life. I need you in my bed and I think you feel the same way."

"Jeremiah, I've been in love with you since ninth grade." She smiled as his head snapped up and her gaze met his.

"You have?"

"Yes. I couldn't figure out a way to get you to see me as a woman who might complete you instead of Callie, your friend at the garage."

"You've always been my friend."

"I know, but I wanted to be more."

"I guess I was too blind to see you in a different light than what I'd seen you in forever. After you started hanging out with other men in front of me, I didn't like how it made me feel. I wanted to tear you from their side and drag you away like some caveman."

She laughed. "So that's where the behavior came from."

He grinned. "You have to admit you kinda like that about me."

"Yeah, I guess I do."

The waiter arrived to take their order, but the moment he left, Jeremiah took her hand again. "We need to decide on where we go from here."

"I know I want to be with you and only you so I think we should date exclusively."

"I agree. I don't want anyone else." His gaze was intense as he said the words. He meant everything, including the I love you. "I love you, Callie."

"I love you too, Jeremiah."

"We should get married." His eyes brightened as a smile spread across his lips.

She pulled her hand out of his grasp and held it up. "Whoa! Take a step back. You're going kind of fast for me."

"Fast? I thought when two people loved each other, they got married."

"Yeah, maybe eventually, but we just started this journey. Let's date for a while before we jump on the marriage bandwagon."

He tilted his head to the side. "Why are you so gun-shy now?"

"I'm not. I just think we should take this kind of slow."

"Okay. I'm with you then. We'll date, go on picnics, go out for dinner, go to movies, you know, all those couple things."

"What changed your mind about me?"

He grasped her hand again. "My mom's accident. I talked to them before it happened about you and me."

"You did?"

"Yeah. She told me to stay away from you."

Frustration and anger zipped through her. *Told him to stay away from her, did she?* "Wow. Really?"

"Yep, but telling a Young to stay away from a woman is like throwing meat on the grill at a barbeque and then telling all the people there they can't have it."

"Okay, blonde moment here, I don't understand. Why did she tell you to stay away from me?"

"Not because she didn't want us together, Callie. My mom knew exactly how I would react to the statement. She knew I'd do the opposite so she was playing a little reverse psychology thing on me. She wants us together, trust me on this."

"Are you sure?"

"Positive." He brought her fingers to his lips, kissing the backs before he continued. "She loves you and would welcome you into the family in a heartbeat, baby."

"Okay."

Their dinner arrived as two steamy plates. Hers was steak and lobster tail where his was a huge ribeye. As they ate in silence, Callie contemplated all Jeremiah had said before dinner. He loved her? Why was she not quite convinced he'd changed his mind too quickly. It seemed too easy to her. Jeremiah rubbed the fingers of his right hand, shaking them like they'd gone to sleep. "What's wrong?"

"My fingers have been going numb. I'm going to make a doctor appointment this week. I've had some other things I'd like to talk to him about to see what I should do."

"Like what?"

"Blurry vision but the numbness mostly." He smiled. "Nothing to worry about. It's a pinched nerve probably. I got bucked off a horse about a month ago."

She frowned. "You could have been seriously hurt, Jeremiah. You should have gone to the doctor when it happened. Please call to make an appointment tomorrow. I'm worried now."

"That's sweet. I like you worried about me."

"I'm serious." She wanted to hit him with her plate. *Stubborn man.*

"Me too. I'll call in the morning. I'll be fine."

She exhaled before picking up her wine glass with a shaky hand to drain the remainder. This scared her more than anything. The blurry vision and numbness could be anything, but since they admitted their love for each other, it meant a whole lot more.

When dinner concluded, they walked out to the truck with their arms around each other as she soaked up being close to him like this.

"Come back to my place. I want to love on you."

"Okay, but I can't stay all night. I have to open the garage tomorrow for Dad. He has a doctor's appointment in the morning."

The frown on his face made her smile. He looked like a lost little boy who'd just had someone take his favorite toy away.

"You'll be fine."

"I want you with me all the time."

"We need to take this relationship slowly. We haven't been a couple until now. This is all new."

"I know, but I want to show you off, be with you, sleep with you, wake up next to you. You know, all the things lovers do." He opened her door, lifted her by the waist, and deposited her on the seat, buckled her seatbelt for her and then leaned in to kiss her on the lips. He shut the door before going around to the driver's side.

As they drove back to Bandera, he held her hand over the center of the truck's console the entire trip. She liked this new relationship they had. It was different and special. She'd always known they would be good for each other. It took him some time to figure it out, but now that he had, everything should be fantastic.

"How is your mom doing?" She frowned. "What happened anyway?"

"She's doing better. A drunk driver hit her on the back road to our ranch the other night, head-on. She had some bleeding on the brain so they put a tube down her throat so they could keep her asleep and make sure she has enough oxygen to her brain. They needed the swelling to go down and the bleeding would hopefully stop on its own. It has and they are going to take out the tube tomorrow. I plan to go in to see her sometime in the afternoon. Do you want to come?"

"I don't think that would be a good idea, Jeremiah. I mean, I'm not family."

"You will be eventually."

"But I'm not right now and don't put the cart before the horse. We might find we can't stand each other once we get to know one another better."

He kissed her fingers. "Not going to happen, sweetheart. I love you."

"You have no idea how much I like hearing you say those words."

"You'll hear them a lot more in the coming years."

"I hope so, but no, you go on and see her. I'll wait until she comes home and gets some rest before I stop by."

"She'll have to have rehab for a bit. She broke her leg too."

"Wow. It's a wonder she wasn't killed."

"The guy would have been a dead man if she had."

"I'm sorry. I don't mean to be morbid. I'm glad she wasn't hurt worse."

He shuddered as he squeezed her fingers. "Me too."

Several minutes later, they pulled up the gate of Thunder Ridge and she waited while he punched in the code to open the gate.

"I love this place."

"Me too."

"I hear there are ghosts on the property."

"Yep. A cowboy, a couple upstairs in the main lodge, and a group of children who play in the yard."

"Have you ever done any research on who they are to maybe find out why they're trapped here?"

"No, but I've thought about it. I hear the children the most since I'm out in the cabin area."

"Do you hear them a lot?"

"Yeah. If it's real quiet you can hear them almost every night, especially if I'm coming in late or something."

"That would kind of freak me out, I think." She shivered at the thought.

"Don't worry. I'll protect you. Besides, they're children."

"I know, but ghosts are ghosts."

They pulled up in front of his cabin. When he shut the engine off, he waited for a minute before coming around to open hers. *Gentleman to the core.*

"You're safe. I don't hear them right now."

"Good."

He swept her up into his arms, carrying her toward the door of his cabin after he pushed the truck door closed with his foot.

"You shouldn't be carrying me."

"Why not? I want to hold you."

"Yeah, but if your back is messed up or something is pinched, you could be hurting yourself more by carrying me."

"I'll take my chances." He reached over to kiss her on the lips before she could say another word. "Reach in my shirt pocket for my keys and open the door."

"Okay."

Once the door was opened, he carried her inside to deposit her on the bed. "Stay there."

She kicked off her heels and tucked her legs beneath her as she watched him shut the door and flip on the light.

His space was so much like him, western décor, wrought iron headboard and footboard, wooden nightstands and a huge computer desk, never mind the big-ass television with a top of the line gaming system. He liked his toys apparently.

"Why are you still dressed?"

"Because I thought you might like the honors of peeling this dress off me."

"Oh, yeah. I could do that."

She stood at the side of the bed as he sauntered closer. "You look so awesome tonight in your dressy gear, but I like the rugged cowboy too."

"You do, huh?"

"Yeah." She watched as he peeled off his jacket and hung it on the back of a chair before he toed off his boots and walked over to stand in front of her in his white shirt, pressed jeans, and socks.

He smoothed his hands over her bare shoulders. "You look hot in that dress, but I want you out of it more."

"Take it off then."

Chapter Twelve

With one hand on the zipper at the back of her dress, he slowly peeled it down until the material stopped right at the curve of her butt. The bodice gapped open at her chest, the only thing holding it up were her arms at her sides. He hooked a finger at the bodice on each side and peeled it down her body until the whole thing fell into a pool at her feet. The strapless bra she wore left little to the imagination as he skimmed his fingertips over the swell of her breast.

"I like these."

"My boobs or my bra?"

"Boobs. They are so pretty." He reached behind her to unhook her bra, letting it fall to the floor too. "I love how the little nipples are standing straight up for me." He cupped her right breast in his palm. "They want me."

"Yes, they do." Her voice came out in a breathless sigh. Wanting him this badly made her hot and cold at the same time. Shivers rolled through her whole body, leaving goose bumps on her skin in their wake.

"Are you cold?"

"No. Excited, yes." She splayed her hands on his chest. "I want you out of these clothes."

"In a minute. I want to worship you."

"Such a sweet talker."

"You know it, darlin'."

"There is my favorite word coming from a cowboy."

"What?"

"Darlin' in that little southern drawl. Makes me so horny."

His hands did a slow crawl from her shoulders to her fingertips before each one cupped a breast again. "You weren't horny already?"

"Oh, hell yes I was, but it makes it worse."

"I'll call you darlin' anytime you want me to."

His lips skimmed over her jawline on their way to the shell of her ear. "I'll remember that." This man knew exactly what to do to ramp her up. He did it so well, she almost wondered where he learned all the little tricks he did with his hands and mouth. She might have to ask him one day so she could thank the woman who had taught him to make love. When he laid her back on the bed, she lifted her arms over her head. She remembered how he liked it when she didn't move while he skimmed her body with his mouth or fingers. Pleasing Jeremiah was her utmost concern.

He hooked two fingers in the waistband of her nylons and panties and shimmied them down her legs until he could peel them off her feet. "Open for me." She spread her legs, giving him an unadulterated view of her pussy. "So wet." He dipped one finger inside her, making her eyes roll back in her head. "Uh-uh. Eyes on me."

Their gazes held as he slowly slid between her thighs and then licked her pussy from slit to clit.

"Ah, God!"

"Mmm."

The vibration of his lips on her clit almost threw her into a climax, but she tamped the need down. She didn't want to come yet. She wanted to hold out as long as possible for the ultimate release. He wasn't having any of her holding back though. He went in for the kill, licking, sucking, and doing little figure eights on her clit in a rapid fashion.

"Jeremiah!" She threw her head back on the comforter as her whole body vibrated and the force of her climax bowed her back.

He seemed pleased with himself as he licked his way up her body until he reached her mouth. The smile on his lips was infectious.

"Good."

"Better than good. Amazing."

"Oh, I like amazing. Shall we try for two?"

"Mmm. Only if it's from you inside me. I want to feel you deep."

"I can handle that." He reached over into the nightstand drawer for a condom, tore it open with his teeth and rolled it on with one hand.

"You are pretty good at that."

"I've had some practice."

"I bet."

A soft moan escaped her lips when his cock found the entrance to her pussy and slowly slid inside. "So good."

"You feel fantastic. I've been waiting weeks for this."

"Only weeks?"

"Since the last time, so yeah, it's been weeks."

She looked up into his soft, pewter-colored eyes. "You haven't been with anyone since we were together?"

"No. I couldn't. I only wanted you."

"Me too."

"I love you, Callie."

"I love you too, Jeremiah. You are my life."

He slowly started to move as she wrapped her thighs around his hips. He softly kissed her nose and her cheeks, taking the wetness of the tears from her face.

"Why are you crying?"

"Because I never thought we'd be here like this. I never thought I'd hear you say those words to me. I've waited so long for you."

"I'm sorry it took me this long to see you for the woman of my dreams."

As he continued his slow assault on her senses, she lost the ability to think of anything beyond Jeremiah and what he was doing to her body. Her nipples pebbled into hard little nubs when he sucked first one before the other, between his lips. His tongue worshipped her body, moving from her lips to her breasts and back again as he slowly pumped his hips, driving his cock in and out of her body.

"Uh, Jeremiah?"

"Yeah?"

"Can you speed it up a bit? You're killing me." He pushed up so he was standing between her thighs, shoved his hands under her hips and slammed his pelvis against hers. Heaven on a hill, he was fantastic when he made love.

"This is fucking." He slowed his pace to a crawl again. "This is making love." He moved a little faster. "I like both. Which do you prefer?"

"I want you to shut up and fuck me."

"Your wish is my command, darlin'." He shoved against her so hard, he had to hold her in place with his hands. "I'm going to fuck you until you scream for me."

"I already did once."

"Do it again."

"Oh, oh, oh." Each thrust hit just the right spot inside her to drive her up the side of the cliff, leaving her hanging on by her fingernails. "A little bit...yes!" Her scream echoed off the walls of his cabin as she hit her climax a second time.

A few uncoordinated thrusts later, Jeremiah groaned as he came apart as well, slumping against her chest in a heap of boneless mass meant to squash her into the bed. She grunted at the weight on her chest. He had to weigh two hundred pounds at least. "I can't breathe."

"Sorry." He slowly slid out of her with a groan before he walked toward the bathroom to dispose of the condom. When he returned, he had a warm wash cloth in his hands to clean her up with.

"You don't have to do that."

"I want to." Before he wiped her off though, he took one finger, dipped it inside her pussy and then smeared the wetness around her back hole. "I want you here too."

"You do?"

"I want you every way possible, darlin'. This is one more fantasy of mine."

"Okay."

"Do you like anal?"

"I love it, actually. It's one of my favorite positions."

He smiled as he wiped her pussy from top to bottom. "Good. Next time."

"And when will there be a next time?"

"Soon. I need you with me always, so yeah, soon."

She pushed herself up on the pillow. "Come here. I want some cuddling."

The minute he sat back against the headboard, she laid her head on his chest and sighed in contentment. This is what she wanted. Just him. Forever. "I hope your mom will be okay."

"I'm sure she will. They said things were going better."

"It must have been terrible to see her in such a state." She shuddered until his hand made some soothing circles, rubbing up and down her arm. "I would hate to see my dad like that."

"You know, I don't think I ever heard what happened to your mom. I just knew she wasn't around."

"She left us when I was three. I don't remember her much. She's only a few faded pictures and memories to me."

"I'm sorry, darlin'."

"It's not a big deal. She contacted me several years ago wanting to be a part of my life, but I wouldn't. I found out she had a drug problem and wanted money. She figured if she got all cozy with me, I would give her some, I guess. I have my dad. That's all I need."

"Well, I'm sure my mother will become the mother you didn't have. She's like that."

Her fingers swirled in the hair on his chest, entwining them together like their hearts belong there. "I'd be more than happy to have your mom become a surrogate mother for me. I love your mom."

"I do too. She's great and now that they are financially secure, their life will get so much better, I think."

"Financially secure?"

"Yeah. I've been investing for them. They have quite a bit of money in the bank now so they don't have to work anymore if they don't want to, but I can't see them doing that. They love this ranch more than any of us. It's their life."

"I bet, but I'm glad they are doing so well." She sifted her fingers through the hair on his chest. "You should be investing for yourself too, since you are so good at it." He grinned, but didn't reply, making her wonder what he might be hiding. She studied his expression for a moment before sitting up on the bed. "I hate to fuck and run, but I should be getting home. I have to work in the morning."

"All right."

He moved to grab his clothes as she stood by the side of the bed to locate her own. After she slipped on her dress without her bra, and nylons, she shoved her feet into her shoes and proclaimed herself ready to go as she grabbed her wrap off the chair where it had landed when they stumbled inside the cabin.

Once he managed to shove his feet into his boots, he grabbed his keys and hat. "Let's get you home then."

* * * *

The next morning Jeremiah peeled open his gritty eyelids to the early sunrise. He had some work to do on the finances this morning before he went into San Antonio to see his mom. Hopefully by the time he got there they would have removed the breathing tube so she could sit up and talk to him. He didn't want to see her like she'd been a few nights ago.

When he threw his legs over the side of the bed and stood, he stumbled, leaning to the left. He grabbed the bedpost to steady himself. His left leg felt numb from the hip down like he'd slept on it. "Okay, this is getting crazy. I really need to call the doctor."

He shook out his leg until the feeling came back and he could walk on it again without falling. *This isn't normal. People my age don't have these kinds of things happen. It's probably a pinched nerve or something.*

After he managed to get dressed, he heard the breakfast bell ring as he grabbed his wallet, hat and truck keys from his nightstand. He glanced back at the bed with a smile, remembering the night before. Callie took his breath away, spread out like a virgin for the offering. *Damn, I have it bad for her and I like it.*

Tugging on the handle, he opened the door. A small group of people were headed to the main lodge for breakfast from the cabin just up the way. A couple of little kids were laughing and pushing each other like he and his brothers used to do when they were young.

"Hey mister, are you a real cowboy?"

"Yes, sir."

"Do you ride horses?"

"All the time. I've even ridden a few who weren't very tame."

"Really?"

"Yep."

"I want to ride a horse."

"Well, tell your mom and dad we have horses available for everyone to ride. My brother Joey will take good care of you if you want to learn to ride. He's a great cowboy."

"How many brothers do you have?" the boy asked as they opened the door to the lodge.

"Eight."

"Wow. I only have one and he's a pain in the ass."

"Aaron Jefferson. I will not have you talking like that!" his mother yelled and Jeremiah smiled.

"Sorry, Mom." The kid grinned at Jeremiah and then took his place in line for food as Jeremiah headed for the coffee in the corner.

Jeff came around the corner with Terri and their boys. He left Terri at the table to grab some coffee himself. "Did you hear from Dad this morning? Have they taken the tube out?"

"He hasn't called. I figured nothing has changed yet."

"I plan to go into town to see her later. I'm hoping she's awake and talking."

Jeff leaned in to talk softly. "Dad told me what you've done with the finances."

"Oh?"

"Yeah." He glanced at Terri as he smiled. "Can you help me do some investing?"

"Sure."

After a minute, he whispered, "Are there really millions in the bank?"

"Yes."

"Wow. How the hell did you do that?"

"Smart investments."

"I would say so." He clapped Jeremiah on the shoulder before he headed to the table to sit next to his girl and their boys.

Jeremiah was glad his brother trusted him enough to ask for financial advice. It meant a lot to him to have a close relationship to his family.

After breakfast, he went into his office to go over the bills and income from the last month at the ranch to see how much more he could safely take to put into investments for his parents. He didn't want to bleed the ranch dry.

The computer screen blurred, making him rub his eyes to bring it back into focus. *That's it. I'm calling the doctor.* He grabbed the office phone from the receiver, pulled out the rolodex of cards he kept and then dialed Dr. Evans' number.

"Dr. Evans' office. How may I help you?"

"Hi. This is Jeremiah Young. I need to make an appointment with Dr. Evans."

"Can I ask what this is concerning?"

"I'm not sick or I don't think so, but I've been having some blurry vision, numbness and tingling in my hands and legs. I fell off a horse about two weeks ago and I want to make sure I didn't pinch a nerve or something in my back since I landed pretty hard."

Once the receptionist made him an appointment for two days later, he hung up the phone so he could go back to work on the financials. He had to get the bills straight this afternoon before leaving to visit his mom.

When he walked into the hospital room several hours later, he was delighted to see his mother sitting up in bed eating some Jello. "You look a lot better than when I saw you a few days ago." He leaned in a kissed her on the cheek. "How do you feel?"

"Like I've been kicked by a horse."

"I'm sure." He took a seat in a chair near the side of the bed. "Are they going to move you to a regular room soon?"

"Yes, later today. I have to have surgery on the leg tomorrow."

"Well, that sucks."

"How are things at home?"

"They are fine, Mom. Don't worry. We've got it."

She patted his hand and then squeezed his fingers. "I know you do, Jeremiah. I'm not worried."

He raised an eyebrow.

"Okay, just a little, but you know me. I can't not worry."

"Jeff is handling the daily things. The rest of us are doing what needs to be done. You just get better."

"Have you heard anything about the man who hit me?"

"Other than he's still in jail, no. He'll be charged with drunk driving at least, but that doesn't carry a lot of weight anymore. He'll probably get probation or some shit." She looked at him with that *mom look*. "Sorry." He squeezed her fingers. "Where is Dad?"

"Out flirting with the nurses, I'm sure. They all know him by name and wave every time he comes into my room."

"He's a personable guy."

"He's a flirt, but I love him anyway." She took another bite of her food before she set the spoon down. "What's happening between you and Callie? Something good, I hope."

"We've come to an understanding that we love each other."

"Fantastic, Jeremiah! I'm so happy for you. You two will be very good for each other, I think."

"I think so too." He rubbed his hand where the fingers had gone numb again.

"What's wrong?"

"I've been having some numbness and tingling in my hands and legs as well as some blurry vision."

"Didn't you fall off a horse a few weeks ago?"

"Yeah." He held up his hand. "Don't say it. I've already made an appointment with the doctor for in a couple of days. I'm sure it's nothing."

"Well, to be safe you need to get checked out."

"I know." He glanced at his watch. "I should go," he said, climbing to his feet. "I know they only allow you five minutes in here."

"So soon?"

"Yeah. I want to drop by Callie's and let her know how you are doing. She was worried."

"Tell her hello for me." She kissed him on the cheek as he leaned in to kiss her. "I love you, Jeremiah."

"I love you too, Mom. I'm sure everything will be fine with the surgery. We'll get you home in a couple of days with some physical therapy and you'll be good as new in a few weeks."

"Grr," she grumbled. "I hate being laid up."

"I know, but at least you're alive."

"Yes. Thank God for watching out for me."

"I'll try to come by again in a couple of days if they haven't let you out by then to give my brothers a chance to visit."

"The nurses have been doing a complete double take with each of you. I think they aren't going to let me leave just because they want the man candy that keeps coming in to see me."

He laughed. "I'll tell everyone to behave themselves."

"You do that."

"See you soon."

"Love you!"

"Love you too."

He drove back to Bandera with lots of things on his mind—from the problems with his visions to his love for Callie. He couldn't wait to bring her into the family even though she seemed reluctant to do it just yet. Fear and uncertainty probably had something to do with it. Really, this had all happened rather quickly so he couldn't blame her at all.

When he pulled into the garage, he parked his truck next to the building and then went around to the open bays where they worked on cars. "Hey, babe!"

"Jeremiah?"

"Yeah, who else calls you babe?"

She laughed as she came out from under the hood of an old Chrysler. "No one, but you I would hope." She gave him a smooch on the lips. "Did you visit your mom?"

"Yes. She's looking a lot better. They'll be doing surgery on her leg tomorrow and she'll have to stay in the hospital a couple of more days, but then she'll be home with rehab, I'm sure."

"Sounds awesome. I'm so glad she's doing better."

"Me too." He leaned in as she twisted a wrench on something under the hood. "Do you want to get some dinner?"

"I can't tonight. I promised my dad I would be home. He hasn't been feeling well."

"Okay." He moved around behind her, kissing her neck before he ran his tongue around her ear. "I'm going to miss you."

She shivered, but tipped her head to the side so he could do more. "I'll miss you too."

"How about tomorrow? We can have dinner and maybe do a movie in town?"

"I can't. I have plans with Mandy, Peyton and Paige. We planned a girl's night out."

"All right, day after tomorrow."

"Sounds good." She turned around in his arms and looped hers around his neck. "Did you make a doctor appointment?"

"Yeah. Day after tomorrow, so we'll go out after my appointment."

"Good. It's important for you to find out what's wrong."

"I know." He moved around to kiss her on the lips. "I'm fine. Don't worry."

"I love you. I'm going to worry."

"Then I'll have to kiss you until you forget to worry." He ran his tongue along the seam of her lips until she opened for him on a moan. As their tongues tangled, he lost himself in her kiss, totally forgetting where they were until someone honked from outside. "Sorry."

She giggled, actually giggled. He thought it was cute. "I'd better get back to work."

With a smack on her butt, he said he'd see her later and headed to his truck.

Man, I love that girl.

Chapter Thirteen

Jeremiah didn't like the look on the doctor's face. He seemed worried. When the doctor worried, he needed to worry too. "We'll need to do some x-rays and tests, Jeremiah. I'm not sure what's going on with you, but I don't think it's a pinched nerve."

"What could it be?"

"There are several things I won't go into right now because I don't want you getting on Google to look up the different diseases. I won't know until next week after we get a CAT scan of your head, do some nerve tests, and get some x-rays of your back just to make sure you don't have a disc out or something. I don't think that's what it is because you don't have pain in your back. You've told me your vision blurs. Those kinds of symptoms along with the numbness and tingling are something we need to look at more closely."

"Thanks, Doc, but you're scaring the hell out of me."

"I'm sorry, but until I know more, I can't give you any more information on things." He patted him on the shoulder. "You'll be okay until we get the tests done. You can get the CAT scan today at the hospital in San Antonio. I've already called to schedule you an appointment. They had a cancellation, so they could get to you in about an hour if you can get there."

"I'll get there, besides, I want to check on my mom. They were supposed to be releasing her today. I haven't heard from my dad."

"I'm glad she wasn't hurt too badly. A broken leg heals. Other more terrifying injuries don't."

"I know what you mean. She was lucky."

"Yes, she was." Jeremiah stood. "Now, go get the CAT scan, make an appointment for the other tests and get those done, then make an appointment to see me next week so we can go over them."

"Thanks, Doc."

"You're welcome, my boy. Tell your family hello for me. Remind them to get their checkups. I know how you boys are about coming in to see me."

"Yeah, only for broken bones and such."

After he thanked the doctor again, he paid his tab before he headed out to his truck. He didn't like thinking about this for another week, but he didn't have a choice, he guessed. At least tonight he could lose himself in Callie for a few hours.

* * * *

When he pulled up to her house two hours and forty-five minutes later, he smiled. Spending the evening with her would erase all the bad thoughts from his mind and heart, leaving only her to fill the void. He climbed out and walked up to the door.

With a quick rap of his knuckles, he heard Callie call out that she'd get it before she opened the door. *Damn*. She looked pretty even in something as simple as a sweater and jeans. "Hi."

"Hi." She pushed open the screen for him as she stepped back. "Come in."

"Thanks." He shut the door behind him before he slipped an arm around her waist and dragged her in for a quick kiss. "You taste amazing."

"It's dinner. I thought I'd cook."

"What'd you make?"

"Lasagna with French bread and salad." She stepped back. "Are you hungry?"

"Starving."

"Good. How about a beer? I have some in the fridge."

"Sounds good to me." He checked out her butt in those jeans as she walked back into the kitchen. *What a nice ass!* She returned a few minutes later with a bottle of beer and a kiss before she went back into the kitchen to finish getting dinner ready.

"How did the doctor go?"

"He didn't tell me much. Just scheduled some tests."

"Like what?" she asked, setting the table with plates.

"CAT scan, blood work, x-rays. You know, the normal stuff."

"Did he say what he thought might be the problem?"

"Not really. He wouldn't tell me his thoughts." He took a sip of the beer in his hand. "He didn't want me looking stuff up on the web and self-diagnosing."

"Smart man."

He chuckled and took another sip. "Yeah. He knows our family well."

Her father came out of the bedroom, limping slightly on his left foot.

"Are you okay, Daddy?"

"Yeah, just my MS acting up again."

"MS?" Jeremiah asked, not sure what that was.

"Multiple Sclerosis. I've had it for years. Makes my limbs go numb so I have to walk with a cane sometimes. It's a bitch of a disease, but I get by."

Jeremiah startled when her father described his symptoms. It sounded just like what he'd been going through. "When were you diagnosed?"

"About fifteen years ago. I take a medication daily to keep the symptoms at bay, but it's hard to manage some days. Today was one of those days." He smiled at Callie. "Thank God for Callie at the garage. She handles the stuff I can't on bad days."

"Wait. Don't you have some of the numbness stuff too, Jeremiah?"

"Yeah, but don't you go telling me I have Multiple Sclerosis. I can't be laid up in a wheelchair or something for the rest of my life. Besides, the doctor didn't mention that. I'm sure if he thought it might be some disease, he would have said something."

She put both her hands on his cheeks. "Just stop. You fell from a horse. We know how that can mess with a person. Don't jump to conclusions just because my dad has some of the same symptoms you've been experiencing." She kissed him and then stepped back but not far enough he'd lose touch with her body. "I love you. It doesn't matter what it is. We'll deal with whatever it turns out to be."

He took several deep breaths to calm his racing heart. He couldn't be sick. He didn't feel sick. He felt fine except for the symptoms. "What if it is?"

"Don't, Jeremiah. Don't freak yourself out." He put her arms around his waist, burying her face in his neck. "I love you."

"I love you too."

"Are you two getting married?"

She shook her head before she reached up and gave Jeremiah a quick kiss on the lips. "No, Dad. This is all new. We are dating for now."

Her father sank down onto one of the dining room chairs, propping his cane up on the table. "Well I'm glad to see you together. You two are cute."

She stepped back from Jeremiah and went back into the kitchen to take the food out of the oven. His mind whirled with questions. He wouldn't drag her into an uncertain future if he had some kind of terrible disease like Multiple Sclerosis. He couldn't. That wouldn't be fair to her. She already had to deal with her dad having it, he wouldn't subject her to a life with a cripple for a husband.

Dinner was a hushed time as Jeremiah reflected on the dire straits of his possible diagnosis. He absolutely refused to tie her down to a man who wasn't a hundred percent healthy, one who could take care of her, not the other way around, one who would be there for her and their children in their time of need, not a shell of a man who couldn't wipe his own ass.

Once dinner was over, he excused himself to leave. He needed to think. Thinking meant alone time even though he wanted nothing more than to kiss her, touch her, hold her, and make love to her.

As he walked out to his truck to go home, she stopped him with a hand on his arm. "Jeremiah, don't leave."

"I need to, Callie. I need some time alone."

"Don't shut me out."

"I'm not."

"Yes, you are. You're thinking way too much about this. Don't. Wait until the doctor tells you what is wrong before you start planning your future. You have no idea what the diagnosis will be and you are doing exactly what he told you not to do. Self-diagnosis is a bad thing. Please? I love you."

"I love you too, but I can't be with you right now."

"Please, don't leave. Don't do this, Jeremiah."

"I'm sorry, but I have to." He leaned in to kiss her lightly on the lips before climbing into his truck and leaving her standing in the driveway.

* * * *

Over the next few days, she called constantly to check on him. Sometimes he answered, other times he let her call go to voicemail. He couldn't face her right now, not until he talked to the doctor, which was today. Hopefully they would have some answers for him so he could move on with his life in whatever capacity that entailed.

He sat nervously in the waiting room of the doctor's office for them to call him into the back. He hated this, hated doctors, hated hospitals, and hated what he was doing to Callie, but he felt the need to protect her even if it was from himself.

"Jeremiah? Come on back," the nurse said.

He climbed to his feet and then she put him in one of those small little waiting rooms to go crazy in. They needed to make the things padded or something.

Lucky for him, the doctor didn't wait too long before coming in to take a seat on one of those little rolling stools.

"We have you test results in, Jeremiah."

"And?"

"I'm afraid it isn't good news. It's not a pinched nerve. I feared the worst and it's not that, so you have to be thankful for the small concession. At first I thought it might be a brain tumor with the symptoms, but it's not. You have something called Multiple Sclerosis. It's a disease process affecting the nerve cells in your brain. It's an auto-immune disease where your immune system attacks the brain cells by mistake, damaging the myelin sheath of your brain, spinal cord, and eyes. When these nerve endings get damaged, it affects your movement and your eyesight."

"Is there a cure?"

"No. I'm sorry, there isn't."

"Fuck."

"There are medications to handle the symptoms. You can even go into remission where you won't have symptoms at all for a long time."

"So I have to be on some medicine for the rest of my life?"

"Yes."

"What is the eventual outcome of this?"

"Everything in our life leads to death, Jeremiah. Some people are completely disabled from this. We won't know what type of MS you have until we've sent you to a neurologist who can study your symptoms and decide the best course of action."

"This isn't fair, you know. I just found the girl of my dreams. My future is set. Now this."

He put a hand on Jeremiah's shoulder. "I know, son. You're in the prime of your life. Don't get too worked up about it yet until you see the neurologist in San Antonio. The guy I'm sending you to is fantastic in this field. He knows his stuff. He'll help you manage things so you'll have the best quality of life."

Dread hit him in the chest like a brick. *What am I going to do about Callie?*

"If you have any general questions I can help you with, don't hesitate to call me. I would suggest making a list of things you would like to ask the specialist before you go so you can make an informed decision about your care. This isn't the end of the world, son. You can lead a normal life for the most part as long as you stay on the medications the doctor prescribes for you. You can still marry, have children, and be the young man you should be right now."

"Thanks, Doc."

"You're welcome. I'll have my nurse make you an appointment with the neurologist. You stay here while she does."

The doctor walked out as a tear slid down his cheek. He couldn't ask Callie to marry him now. He wouldn't make her deal with this. Better he cut it off right now and save her the pain.

The nurse came in a few minutes later as he angrily wiped the wetness from his face. Men didn't cry and he wasn't going to let himself break down again.

"Here is your appointment card with the neurologist. It's set for Monday."

"That's fine. Thank you."

"You can stay in here as long as you like. Gather your thoughts, but just remember, this isn't the end of the world. People are diagnosed with this disease all the time. They go on to live happy, healthy, and productive lives. You're still young. You can handle this." She smiled softly and walked back out the door, leaving him alone.

He sat in his truck for several long minutes as his mind raced from one subject to another and back. Callie was at the forefront of his thoughts though while he tried to decide what to do. He'd already pushed her away, trying to save her the heartache of living with a man who wasn't whole, but he would have to tell her the diagnosis and live with her anger as he shut her out of his life for good.

* * * *

Callie waited for Jeremiah at Anne's diner. He'd called her on his way home from the doctor's office to say he wanted to see her. She was surprised he'd picked here, somewhere in public. They should be alone for this, she figured, but apparently he didn't think so.

When she saw him walked through the door, she smiled. *Damn, he looked good, tall, broad-shouldered, and tough.* Whatever this was wouldn't tear them apart. She wouldn't let it.

He slid into the booth seat across from her and took her hand in his. He closed his eyes as his lips brushed her palm. Her heart did a little staccato rhythm at the touch of his mouth. He could totally turn her inside out with nothing more than a look or a touch.

"Hi."

"Hey."

"Why did you want to meet here?"

"I figured it was best."

"Best for whom?"

"Us."

"Why?"

"Hey, kids. Can I get you anything?" Anne stopped at their table with a bright smile.

"I'll take a Coke," Callie replied as Jeremiah shook his head.

"Be right back."

After Anne brought her drink and Callie retrieved her hand reluctantly from Jeremiah's grasp, she sat back in the seat waiting for his words to start flowing.

"We need to break this off."

"Break what off?"

"Our relationship. I don't want to see you anymore."

"What the fuck, Jeremiah? You can't just shut me down like this."

"I can and I will to protect you."

"Protect me from what? You aren't making sense." Trepidation ripped through her at the look in his eyes. He wasn't kidding. The seriousness of his expression made her angry. *Stubborn man!* "I won't let you do this. Whatever it is—"

"It's MS, Callie."

"So?"

"I can't." He shook his head. "I won't let you live your life with a man who can't be a hundred percent for you. You already have to deal with your father having this terrible disease and now your future husband?"

"You will *not* make that decision for me. I've lived with my dad's disease for the last several years. I've seen what it can do and I'm not afraid of it." She grabbed his hand, but he pulled it back out of her reach. "I love you, Jeremiah. Why can't you understand that? Why can't you see it doesn't matter to me? You are my life."

"I refuse to strap you to a man who won't be able to take care of you."

She slapped her hand on the table causing him to jump. "I don't care, you stubborn jackass! But if you want to turn your back on our love because you're afraid, then so be it, but don't use the excuse you don't want to strap me with a crippled man because that isn't going to fly. Loving you means we are together forever no matter what. Obviously you don't love me enough to want to be with me." She leaned in with her elbows on the table. "What if I had MS? Would you turn your back on me?"

He shook his head and refused to look her in the eye. "No. I would be there for you."

"Then why are you pushing me away?" she asked, fear making her all the more angry because he wouldn't face that they were meant to be together. "We can fix this. Don't let us die. The love of a lifetime is worth at least a million tries. What we've got is too good for good-bye."

When he looked back up, she could see the terror, loneliness, and desperation in his gaze. "Don't you see? I'm supposed to be the one taking care of you, not the other way around."

"Listen to yourself. You can justify it all you want to in your head, but it's not going to work. One-sided love isn't for me. If you love me, you'd see this is crazy talk, Jeremiah. Please, don't shut me out."

"I'm sorry, Callie. I refuse to put you through this." He got out of the booth and walked out without another word.

Tears welled up in her eyes as she watched him leave. *How can he do this? How can he turn his back on me? I thought he loved me.*

Anne came over and sat down next to her, wrapping her in a one-armed hug as she cried ugly, sobbing tears into her shoulder.

"He'll come around, honey. He's a Young. They do this kind of thing."

"What am I going to do?"

"Give him time. He's in shock, I'd imagine. I also know Jeremiah is one of most stubborn of the boys, and that is saying a lot because the whole lot of them are stubborn. He's about the most like his momma out of all of the boys. She's got the stubborn streak down to a science. Trust me." She patted Callie's shoulder as she reached for a napkin to dry her tears.

"Thanks, Anne."

"You're welcome, honey. If you want to talk, you call me."

"I will, but right now I think I need to talk to Peyton and Paige. They are married to two of the brothers. They might know more about how to handle this than anyone."

"I'm sure they can help, but remember, I'm here for you."

Callie dug out her phone to call her friends to meet her at her house in an hour. Peyton, Paige and Mandy all converged on her living room with wine, chocolate, chips, and cookies to discuss this new development.

"I need you all to promise not to tell your husbands about this. I don't know if Jeremiah has told his brothers what's going on or not. I don't want to break his confidence. This concerns me and him right now."

Peyton nodded as Paige replied, "Okay."

"Jeremiah has been diagnosed with Multiple Sclerosis." She went on to tell them what she knew about the disease, how her father had it as well, and how things progressed if left unchecked by medication. She explained all she knew about the disease before she went on to tell them about her conversation with Jeremiah at the diner. "I don't know what to do. He's shut me out."

Mandy sat forward on the chair, resting her elbows on her knees. "I didn't realize you two were even serious, but he's being a typical Young from what I know about the family."

"True," Peyton added. "It sounds very much like what my husband would do."

"Mine too." Paige put in her opinion, which is exactly what Callie thought they would say.

"What am I going to do?"

"Give him time," Peyton said. "He needs to come to grips with the diagnosis first. Let him talk to the neurologist and find out his life isn't over because of this disease. He'll come around."

"God, I hope so. I wanted to punch him."

They all laughed as Paige replied, "I bet you did. He's worse than some of the other brothers in his stubbornness. I think it comes from handling all the family finances. He has to be such a hard-ass to be able to tell them no they can't buy a new horse or purchase a new fifty thousand dollar tractor."

She swiped at the tears on her cheeks, sniffing to clear her plugged nose. "Thanks everyone. I knew I could count on you three to help me."

"Honey, you know we are here for you no matter what. We all know what dealing with those boys is like," Mandy said even though she didn't have a brother herself yet.

"Shall we watch some sappy movie tonight?" She looked at Paige. "What did you do with the twins tonight?"

"Daddy is watching them for a change."

"Wow, I bet that is interesting."

"He does pretty well with them. They're getting so big, they're two little terrors on the loose, but he's such a sucker for their little smiles and cuteness."

"What's he going to do when Hannah starts dating?"

"He won't even talk about that right now."

"How are you and Jason doing? Any baby news yet?"

"Oh, hell no. We are waiting for a bit before we start trying for a little one."

"I bet Grandma isn't happy about that."

"She already has enough grandchildren for now. She can wait a few more years."

"How is she taking being laid up at home with the broken leg?"

"Not well. She wants to be up and doing this and that, although we have managed to get her into her office so she can handle some stuff even with a broken leg. She's doing well with the rehab though. The physical therapist is coming out three times a week to work with her."

"That's great. I was so worried when I heard about her accident."

"As we all were."

The rest of the evening passed with the girls getting pretty drunk, laughing at their men, and just spending quality time with each other. Callie needed this, needed the companionable silence as they watched *The Notebook* on television and cried big, ugly tears. The cleansing feeling of being with like-minded women, helped her to understand Jeremiah's feelings and let him go to find his own way, so he could find his way back to her.

Chapter Fourteen

Callie decided to confront Jeremiah after his neurologist appointment on his own turf with his brothers watching. She managed to get Peyton and Paige to gather the brothers as well as his mother and father in one of the lodge's main rooms. He hadn't told them about the disease yet that the girls could fathom so she wanted them to confront him with that fact too.

As she drove to the ranch, fear gripped her. What if this backfired? What if he got angry with her for doing this?

When she'd made this plan, she really hadn't thought of the consequences of her actions, but what could it hurt? He'd pushed her out of his life anyway, so pressing him more couldn't hurt any worse.

When she pulled into the front of the lodge, Peyton stood outside waiting for her.

"Ready?"

"As I'll ever be, I guess."

"The boys are all in the main room. We've put a sign on the door to keep the visitors out until this is over. Jeremiah is in his cabin. Jeff went to get him." She put her arm around Callie. "I did tell him what was going on so he knew why the secrecy and the meeting. He's pissed that Jeremiah didn't tell them, but he understands. He's on your side."

"Good."

When they walked into the lodge, every eye turned toward her. She could see the questions on their faces and in their eyes, but she had to wait to confront Jeremiah.

Jeff practically dragged him into the room several minutes later.

"What the hell is this all about?"

"Why don't you tell us, Jeremiah?"

"I don't know what you are talking about."

"You went to the doctor. Tell us what is going on so we can help you."

Jeremiah's gaze swung to her as she stood in the corner waiting for him to speak. "It's nothing."

"Bullshit. Spill it."

Jeremiah inhaled before he forcibly exhaled. "I have Multiple Sclerosis."

"What is that?" Jackson asked.

"It's an auto-immune disease affecting the nerves in my brain. I went to the neurologist today. He started me on a medication which is supposed to dull the symptoms and make it easier to deal with. Basically, it makes my limbs go numb at times and messes with my vision. For now, those are the symptoms, but eventually it could put me in a wheelchair."

Jeff put his arm around him. "We are here for you, Jeremiah. No matter what. You know that."

The other brothers did the same as they all got together in a group to give him the support he needed. It brought tears to Callie's eyes. She knew they would react this way. Now only if she could convince Jeremiah they belonged together. "I need to say something, please, and I hope you all will bear with me for interrupting your family time, but I feel this is important to say in front of you so you can beat him over the head in my defense." She stepped toward the group. "Jeremiah and I have been seeing each other. We have professed our love for one another a couple of weeks ago, but when he got the diagnosis of this disease, he shut me out claiming he didn't want to burden me with a cripple for a mate. My father has this disease as well. I've been living with it for several years. I know what it can do. I've done the research and I want him to realize it doesn't matter to me. He's my life. Please help me convince him we belong together no matter what life brings."

"What's this all about, Jeremiah?" his mother asked from her wheelchair off to the side of the group.

"I don't want to stick Callie with a cripple for a husband, Mom. I refuse to do that to her."

"She loves you and you love her, right?"

"Yes."

"Then quit being a dumbass and ask that girl to marry you."

"But—"

"But nothing. Life is short. We never know when we'll leave our loved ones behind. I've learned this myself the last several weeks as I saw your father and you boys deal with my accident. I could have been killed. I know it would have left you all devastated, but it's not something we can control. If you love her, then cherish the time you have together by being together and loving each other like your life depends on it."

Callie watched as Jeremiah turned back toward her. His grey eyes reflected love and acceptance as the words from his mother finally sank in.

Jeremiah stepped out of the circle of his brothers to approach her, taking her hand in his as he stopped in front of her. "I'm sorry, Callie. I do love you, but I'm scared."

"I know, Jeremiah. I am too. I don't want to lose you. I don't want to have to deal with your disease, but I'm a strong woman who knows how to handle adversity no matter how much you want to protect me. I love you."

"I love you too. I'm so sorry I put you through this." With tears shining in his eyes, he got down on one knee. "I don't have a ring for you right this minute, but will you marry me?"

She got down on the ground so they were face to face. She grasped his cheeks in her hands as she whispered a exuberant, "Yes!" She threw herself into his embrace, kissing him all over his face while he laughed.

His brothers slapped him on the back in congratulations until she managed to get him down on the floor, lying across his chest.

"This is a precarious position, darlin'. Not that I mind, you see, but I don't think you are into exhibitionism, are you?"

"Jeremiah!"

He laughed as he rolled her under him and kissed her full on the mouth. When they came up for air, the room had cleared of his family. He threaded his fingers in her hair, bringing one small bunch around to tickle her lips. "I love you."

"I love you too. When do you want to get married?"

"I don't care. I want something small though. Only a few friends and family."

"Sounds good to me." A twinkle in his eyes told her he was up to something. "Ever been to Hawaii?"

"Nope."

"Let's get married there. I can fly everyone out there. We'll have a wedding on the beach."

"I love that idea, but how can you afford to fly everyone out there? Won't it be really expensive?"

"We need to talk about finances, darlin', but don't worry, I can afford it and then some."

"If you say so. I'll leave that to you."

"Trust me when I say you won't have to worry about money for the rest of your life."

"Are you rich?"

"Let's say comfortable." He kissed her full on the mouth, letting his tongue slide along the seam of her lips in an erotic dance until she opened for him on a groan.

When they parted, she said, "We are going to have to find somewhere else to live. Although I love your little cabin, there isn't room for both of us."

"I'm already planning on a house on the hill overlooking the valley. I'll show you the plans after we make love."

"Oh, I like the sound of that."

"Good." He climbed to his feet and held out a hand to her, dragging her up before he tossed her over his shoulder to head to his room.

"Jeremiah?"

"Yeah."

"This caveman behavior is perfect."

He laughed all the way to the cabin as her hair hung down his back and her hand had a firm grip on his buttocks.

Epilogue

Orange and red streaked the sky, making the sunset spectacular as they sat on the lounge near their cabana on Maui.

Jeremiah kissed her forehead when she snuggled down into his embrace, admiring the rock on her left hand. She couldn't believe they were actually married.

The ceremony had been beautiful. He'd been dressed in a pure white pair of pants, white shirt, white cowboy hat with no shoes as she approached him in her off-the-shoulder white gown and bare feet. Clutched in her shaking hands was a bouquet of roses, lilies and baby's breath tied with a deep blue ribbon.

His family and her father had stood by as she stopped next to him to take his hand in hers.

When all was said and done, she whispered her new name in awe, not quite believing she'd actually married her Jeremiah.

"What are you thinking about?"

"You. The ceremony. Everything. It's hard for me to believe we are actually here in Hawaii and married. I've waited so long for this."

"I love you, Callie."

"I love you too." She sighed as she ran her fingers through the hair on his chest. "When is the house getting started?"

"Next week. They're breaking ground for the foundation while we're here. Dad is keeping an eye on them after he and mom get back from here."

"It was so great to have our families here for this. It was perfect."

"I only want what my wife wants." She sat up and gave him the most dubious look she could muster. "What?"

"Somehow I doubt that."

"Why would you say something like that? I only want what you want."

"Because I know how stubborn you can be, Jeremiah. Somehow I don't think I'll be getting away with much of anything."

He wrapped an arm around her and pulled her back down to his chest. "You have me wrapped around your little finger, Mrs. Young. Don't think any different."

"What happens when we have kids?"

"They'll have me wrapped around their fingers too, I'm sure, just like their mother."

"Especially if we have little girls."

"Oh, definitely."

"How soon do you want children?" His fingers did a slow crawl down her arm, sending shivers racing in their wake.

"I'm not in any hurry. Are you?"

"Not really. I want to have some time, just the two of us, before we jump into having a family."

"How many kids do you want?"

"I want a big family. Lots of kids, like six. I was lonesome as a child. I don't want our kids to be like that."

"Sounds good to me."

"Are you going to ever tell me exactly how much money is in the bank?"

"Are you curious?"

"Yeah, but that's not the reason I married you. You can handle all the bills and money. As long as I have an allowance to buy groceries, I'm good."

"Honey, you can buy the entire store and it won't hurt our finances."

"How much, Jeremiah?"

He laughed as she ran her fingernail around his nipple. "Current balance or in general?"

"General figure is fine."

"We have over ten million in the bank."

She choked on her saliva as she muttered, "Ten million?"

"Yeah, and it's growing every day."

"Holy shit."

"So when we get back, if you want to close your dad's garage, you can. I'd rather like not having you work."

"But I like working at the garage."

"I know you do, baby, that's why I wouldn't ask you to, unless you wanted to."

"I'll talk to my dad to see what he says. I'd like to set him up so he wouldn't have to worry about anything ever again. He could have someone come in to help him since I won't be there anymore on a regular basis."

"Done."

"I love you, Jeremiah. You are so good to me."

"You are the best wife a man could ask for." He pushed her onto her back and ran his tongue from her shoulder to her ear. "Wanna make love?"

"I thought you'd never ask."

The End

About the Author

Sandy Sullivan is a romance author, who, when not writing, spends her time with her husband Shaun on their farm in middle Tennessee. She loves to ride her horses, play with their dogs and relax on the porch, enjoying the rolling hills of her home south of Nashville. Country music is a passion of hers and she loves to listen to it while she writes.

She is an avid reader of romance novels and enjoys reading Nora Roberts, Jude Deveraux and Susan Wiggs. Finding new authors and delving into something different helps feed the need for literature. A registered nurse by education, she loves to help people and spread the enjoyment of romance to those around her with her novels. She loves cowboys so you'll find many of her novels have sexy men in tight jeans and cowboy boots.

Other books by Sandy

Love Me Once, Love Me Twice (Montana
Cowboys 1)
Before the Night is Over (Montana Cowboys 2)
Two for the Price of One (Montana Cowboys 3)
Difficult Choices (Montana Cowboys 4)
Doctor Me Up (Montana Cowboys 5)
Stakin' His Claim
Country Minded Cougar
Meet Me in the Barn
Taming the Cougar
The Call of Duty Anthology
Five Hearts Anthology
Trouble With a Cowboy
Gotta Love a Cowboy
Make Mine a Cowboy (Cowboy Dreamin' 1)
Healing a Cowboy's Heart (Cowboy Dreamin' 2)
For the Love of a Cowboy (Cowboy Dreamin' 3)
Tempted by the Cowboy (Cowboy Dreamin' 4)

Secret Cravings Publishing
www.secretcravingspublishing.com

www.ingramcontent.com/pod-product-compliance
Lightning Source LLC
Chambersburg PA
CBHW070826120626
46556CB00002B/668